Enthusiastic reviews for Lior Samson's novels –

Distant Sons

" [A] book that will stay with me, probably for the rest of my life, and that I know I'll read again. ... It enlarged my experience of being human." — *M. Thornberg, author*

The Rosen Singularity

" The plotting is ingenious and the characters come through strongly." — *Rebecca Goldstein, MacArthur Fellow, author*

The Millicent Factor

" A solid page turner. The author keeps the pace just right with action and chases ... and backroom dealings." — *RJ Beam, author*

The Intaglio Imprint

" Super-realism and compelling rationale, ... an intricate and incisive creation." — *George Church, geneticist*

The Drucker Proxy

" An edge-of-the-seat, emotionally gripping, intimate, arousing, techno-legal tour-de-force." — *Phillip M. Samson, attorney*

Bashert (The Homeland Connection)

" Samson writes with a crisp elegance, like John Le Carré, and weaves his plot magically." — *James A. Anderson, author*

The Dome (The Homeland Connection)

" An excellent read, and very highly recommended." — *Midwest Book Review*

Web Games (The Homeland Connection)

" This extraordinary author has the ability to anticipate events. ... You will not put it down." — *Alan Caruba, critic, BookViews*

Chipset (The Homeland Connection)

"[A] multi-dimensional thriller ... populated by flesh-and-blood characters."
- Avraham Azrieli, author

Gasline (The Homeland Connection)

"[A] great novel . . . high concept, flesh-and-blood protagonist, and realistic action. ... [It] will raise your blood pressure and make you think."
– Columbia Review of Books and Film

Flight Track (The Homeland Connection)

"Stunning, compelling, thought-provoking. To the book's broad scope and expert pacing, add three-dimensional, engaging characters."
– M. Thornburg, author

Exit Plans (The Homeland Connection)

"Page-turner, nail-biter, thought-provoker [by] one of the two great American writers of near-future-maybe-as-soon-as-tomorrow fiction most worth reading ."
– M. Thornburg, author

The Four-Color Puzzle

"[A]n authentic thinking person's ideal mystery; an eloquent feast of words and an excellent story."
– Jeanie B. Clemmons, author

The
DOME

Tenth Anniversary Edition

The DOME

a novel by Lior Samson

GESHER PRESS

Gesher Press | Ampersand Press
Rowley, MA 01969

Printed in the United States of America.
5 4 3 2 1

ISBN 978-1-7326091-6-7

Cover and book design: Larry Constantine
Cover and interior photos: Jörg Behmann, by permission
Set in Bodoni MT and Bodoni MT Black

To Devan, my multitalented son,
who keeps teaching an old dog new tricks.

What is objectionable, what is dangerous about extremists,
is not that they are extreme, but that they are intolerant.
The evil is not what they say about their cause,
but what they say about their opponents. – Robert Kennedy

Table of Contents

Preface:

Tenth Anniversary Edition

Preparing a tenth-anniversary edition of *The Dome* affords an opportunity not only for fixing up some of the slips in the original printing but also for looking back into how the book came about. The impetus and inspiration for a story is often a story in itself. My first novel, *Bashert*, completed in 2007 and published in 2010, grew directly out of a real episode from my college days. This sequel had a very different genesis, beginning with my then school-age son who liked the characters I introduced in *Bashert* and urged me to turn them into a "franchise." Now a professional in the music business, he has always had a flair for finding ways to combine his creative and entrepreneurial drives.

However, even the best of characters need a story to occupy, and in this case, the story began as the concept for a screenplay. My wife and I spent our first date with dinner and a movie, and over the twenty-five-plus years since have continued to have a special connection with cinema, not only enjoying good films, but delighting in their deconstruction, taking them apart to understand what makes them work—or not.

From criticism we moved on to construction, exploring original ideas for new films we thought should and could be made. We were a well-matched pair in our screenplay pastime. She has a gift for plotting and motivation, and I have a flair for visualizing settings and scenarios. At one point, I even entertained hope that we might collaborate as screenwriters, but, while my path took me ever deeper into fictional realms, hers took her steadily forward into the factual world of a working research scientist.

The essence of *The Dome* emerged from a dinner-table discussion about the nature of extremism and its role in the ongoing political and religious struggles in the Middle East. We wondered whether there could ever be a way out of the battles for such places as the Temple Mount in Jerusalem, small bits of territory with outsized symbolic significance. We fantasized about how various sorts of extremists might attempt to settle the issue once and for all, then sketched out a plot for a movie.

It should not be surprising, therefore, that readers have remarked on the often cinematic quality of much of my writing. In fact, a New York based screenwriter has written and pitched a screenplay for *Bashert*, and another of my novels, *The Drucker Proxy*, is under consideration by a Hollywood producer.

I am abetted in the writing process by the way my mind works. I am a visual thinker. In my other life, as an industrial designer specializing in safety-critical systems, I often begin working out a design problem by painting a mental picture of the system and imagining a user interacting with it. I may play through several imagined iterations in the design even before I start sketching out ideas on paper, a whiteboard, or my monitor screen.

In writing, I often start by picturing settings and context and by watching a mental movie as a scene plays out. I can see and hear my characters as they cope with the situations in which I place them. At times, I even get into discussions and arguments with them over what they might do next or how a scene might play out. Then I hit the keyboard with my less-than-ten-fingered typing technique to try and convey what I already know and have seen.

The final word is still usually shaped by my erstwhile cowriter, who somehow makes room in her busy professional schedule to read and review the multiple incarnations of my manuscripts and to tell me where I missed the mark. The result here is very different from our original cinematic treatment, not least because that dinner-table version was not peopled with those characters who would later come to life in *Bashert*. I hope you enjoy the amalgam.

Acknowledgements

I am, no surprise, indebted to many people for helping to bring this story to the light of print. First and foremost, to my wife and partner, Lucy, who allowed me to commandeer and find a home for a screenplay concept that we had been batting around for some years, and who suffered through the awkward early iterations of my novel interpretation. I am, once again, grateful to Jim Hawkins and David Tutleman, good friends and good critics who were, as always, unstinting in their support and suggestions. For setting me straight and saving me from embarrassment on several counts, I thank Haifa native Yoram Chisik. I also thank my ever-patient editor, Peter Gordon, for his enthusiasm, his intelligent reviews, and his unflagging encouragement.

I will not list all of those among my family and friends who have believed in me and urged me on as I struggled to persist, but you know who you are and you know I have treasured your support.

The
DOME

Prologue

They were the Sage, the Wizard, and the Wonk. They had all agreed on the need to have code names, but when it came to the reality, or unreality, of assigning them, only the Sage had managed to keep a straight face. On Gmail they had become sage40, wizard423, and wonk88, the ultimate in undistinguished anonymity, anonymity multiplied, forty-fold or 423-fold or 88-fold, although they availed themselves of email only on the rarest of occasions, having established other, more sophisticated channels of communication. When the Wonk chose his handle, the Wizard told him he had spent much too much time watching American TV. She would have preferred literary references: Pangolad, Asinoril, and Shimji, but the Sage had vetoed these for what he said were patently apparent reasons.

It was time, their final meeting. The Sage watched sweet-sour smoke from his cigar drifting up in a lopsided vortex as the door to his study opened. "So good of you to come," he said to the Wizard, gesturing to the open chair opposite. "You know the Wonk, of course." He was clearly having fun.

She laughed. "Yes, and so good to see you again, your Wonkship. And you are looking well, my Sage, my liege. As always." She smiled, a careful and oddly pinched smile that narrowed her broad mouth.

The Sage, controlling the moment with his silence, nodded to her, took a short puff on his cigar, and pursed his thick lips as he studied the two of them, his invited intruders. The small, book-lined study, with its dark Oxonian paneling and immense wingback chairs, was his retreat from the world, his fallout shelter from what he had described, in one of his many essays on the failings of the world, as "the irrational radiation, the din that passed for discourse in the disorder of our modern society."

It was a retreat reserved for him, his books, his cigars, and the more than occasional cognac. He rarely invited anyone into his sanctum sanctorum, but these two were exceptions. His opinions he would share without invitation with anyone in the street or on campus, his thoughts he broadcast on paper to the world, but it was only with these chosen few that he would confess the dark dreams that drove his ideas.

"Matters have become so depressing in your sliver of a country," he said to the Wizard. "I must say I cannot fathom how or why you put up with it."

"My adopted country," she corrected. "We cope. Sometimes it is better, but sometimes, these times, it is worse. Perhaps we need a new vision." She winked at him broadly.

"Vision is a euphemism of modern management for upper echelon proposals in the absence of plans," he said in his best Alistair Cook voice. "It is such a limp word of vague voice, so cerebral and devoid of passion, don't you think? Specification would be a preferable term. Or initiative, perhaps, which has the ring of intention about it. Wouldn't you agree?" He had the sublimely civil but domineering manner of a lifelong academic, a man used to intimidating students and other lesser beings, one who expected to be challenged but never to be wrong.

The Wonk, his junior in both years and position, started to say something, but the Sage continued, as if not wanting a meticulously planned introductory lecture to be interrupted prematurely by some overeager young student. "We," he said with a sweep of his head, "could be the beginning of a change in the course of history. We can offer an opportunity for changing the conversation, for injecting a new subtext into the historic narrative. Please, no visions for me. The time for vision ended with the second intifada. Now is the time for initiative, initiative undergirded by intelligence and discipline." Even now, here, with his closest confidants, he indulged his penchant for pedantry.

His guests both nodded, although the Wizard struggled to suppress a smirk. She had always been amused by his posturing, which had no doubt contributed to both the heat of their early ardor as well as the chill of their later falling out. He sent her a disapproving look, then picked up the newspaper from beside his chair and laid it on the glass-top table, open to inside-page headlines about the latest wave of violence in Jerusalem and the West Bank.

"These times, yes. I am sure you know the story already, all too well. This particular time," he said, tapping on a photo, "it was yet another round of tit-for-tat destruction, with homes in a Jewish settlement in the West Bank shelled by rocket-propelled grenades following the bulldozing of two Palestinian houses alleged to have belonged to the relatives of a 16-year-old martyr, a suicide bomber who had, in her pious but ignorant ineptitude, managed to kill herself while only injuring the right-wing rabbi who was, so it is surmised, her target.

"Of course, there was what our American colleagues prefer to euphemize as 'collateral damage,' in this instance seven students from a Greek tour group who picked the wrong day to visit local churches and synagogues. The attack on the rabbi was, in turn, preceded by the killing of a mullah by mercenaries supposedly, if we are to believe Hamas, in the pay of the Israeli intelligence services.

"Does no one do their own dirty work anymore? Are all fights by proxy? Has impersonal Semtex replaced the assassin's intimately personal shiv?" He took another puff on his cigar, clearly enjoying his rhetorical rant. "All this, of course, consequent to the September riots over new restrictions on access to the attractions," he said, spitting out the word, "on the Temple Mount. The sacred Temple Mount—sacred to the Jews, to Islam, and to Christendom. So we kill each other over it, that it may once again be the cause and sometime site for blood sacrifice. And where does it stop? When do they learn, these benighted barbarian bigots?" No one spoke as he savored his own alliterative outburst, smiling and squinting one eye slightly as though he might be considering a revision to a line in a book manuscript.

6

"I still do not see," he continued, "how anyone as intelligent and rational as you, my Wizard love, could bear to live and work in a theocracy, a country dominated by dark-age denizens like the *haredim*. The orthodox right even call the shots on who is a Jew and who a gentile, who may return and who may not."

The Wizard chewed her lip before speaking. "I work with intelligent and rational people on fast and powerful computers. The ultraorthodox are not much of a factor in our everyday lives."

"Yet they reap even though they do not sow. Their scholars live off the labors of others while holding an entire nation hostage to their archaic standards. But," he said, with a dismissive wave of his hand, "These are obsolescent political and religious matters, that I would hope would soon be utterly obsolete, a hope I have held for what begins to seem like a lifetime.

"I do believe that the Middle East needs more than vision or hope. It needs action of a new order. It is a system, a perpetual motion machine, a self-feeding cycle of death and destruction."

The others nodded with him, slowly and sadly, at first. But they also recognized one of his favorite words and, as they sensed what was coming next, amused smiles spread on their faces.

"Systems, yes," he said. "And who better understands systems? Here we are, if you will forgive my immodesty, three of the most gifted people on the planet—a wizard, a wonk, and a sage—experts on science and politics and political science, and most of all, on systems. It is past time that the likes of us should put our minds to the task of what might be done, the course of action to a new course, an initiative." Now both of his companions, amused by his all too familiar grandiosity, were grinning. Pushing aside the newspaper, he placed three large snifters on the table between them and started to pour from a decanter.

The Wonk waved a dark hand over the nearest glass. "Thank you, no. You know that we ... we don't imbibe."

"Ah, yes, of course. How quaint. Laudable, I suppose, but still quaint." He finished pouring the other two glasses and raised his. "So, then, let us toast to our little political science project, our ... our initiative."

Their gathering at last shifted from monologue to dialogue, and the discussion quickly picked up in pace, ranging widely over many details and no few digressions—on the surface, a medley of intellectual debates, an academic pursuit, but with a smoldering subtext that crackled like static electricity. They talked of finances and logistics, of facilities and personnel, of responsibilities and communication. They reviewed the research already completed and the projects newly funded. They argued over technology and tactics. They highlighted the holes in their insight and expertise and talked of where and from whom and how they might secure what they needed. They reviewed and reiterated until all the issues had been laid bare, the action items had been identified, their ownership designated, and the whole had been committed to memory, since the Sage had declared there would be no notes from any of their meetings.

It was already early morning hours when the Wizard and the Wonk finally took their leave. The Sage, without rising, looked up at them as they stood to go. "You seem, perhaps, reticent, shall we say," he said, looking at the Wizard.

She looked back at him, lips pursed, uncertainty in her eyes. "No, I am with you. I think it is both needed and righteous, if I may be permitted to use such a word. But it is my country, my family, even if I am an adopted child, and I cannot deny my mixed feelings. Nevertheless, that will not keep me from doing my part."

The Sage raised his glass. "All right then, we have our work ahead. I trust you both can see yourselves out. But first, what is it the Jews say? Next year in Jerusalem? So be it, indeed. Next year in Jerusalem. Ah, yes, and that other perennial favorite of modern Israelites, a promise so often invoked even if so seldom kept. Never again!"

His guests long gone, the Sage sat alone in the silence of the study, swirling the last drops of cognac in the bottom of his glass. So much beauty in the world, he thought. He closed his eyes and pictured the cliffs at Ga'ash in Israel, remembering the brilliant light, the on-shore wind steady and strong, and in the sky, a lone kite, climbing and climbing toward the sun, toward the light. I must return. I will. Next year in Jerusalem. Indeed, so much beauty. But also so much ugly stupidity as well. But we shall see what can be done about some piece of that.

Part One

1

The warehouse smelled of machine oil and rain and mold-rotted cardboard. Miserly light from the street filtered through dirt-clouded windows and glistened off greasy pools of water on the heavily stained concrete floor. Hamadi el-Masri, dressed in jeans and a bomber jacket, paced in long-legged strides as they talked. His thick beard had been trimmed in the close-clipped style of the younger men in his employ so that he might stand out less as he crisscrossed the continent and closed deals with infidels. The ropy scar on his chin, where an Israeli bullet had grazed him as a boy, was uncovered. Instead of the pride he had felt at the time, now it made him feel exposed and irrationally vulnerable.

He hated the fat, pale men he was dealing with as much as they hated him, but business was business. The asking price was too high, but it was worth something to get so much from one source, and Hamadi knew they were running out of time and options. Besides, the money was not his money, though some part of it would become his. It was more money than he had ever known, yet still, he was not tempted by it as others were and would be. To him, it was only a means to an end, a greater end: the Sword of the Prophet. He closed the deal with a nod of his head.

"We cannot take care of delivery, of course," the Colonel told him. "The transport you will have to arrange. But you can pick up the material tomorrow night, if you are ready. The warehouse will be guarded by our people, and two of my men will be at the border. There will be no trouble. After that, it's your affair."

"Delivery, transport, these are no problem," Hamadi answered with noticeable impatience. "There is never a shortage of mules. Just be sure it is all in small enough packages as was specified."

"Why must you complicate things? Do you realize what it involves to repackage that stuff? It is not like dividing up soap powder. No, we do not have the time, and I really do not want to put my men at risk."

"That's the deal, Colonel Glinkov. You are already being well compensated. We need packets that can be slipped under a burqa or into a backpack, not barrels that require a truck. You have the people and equipment that can handle it. Half kilogram packages, sealed, wrapped in lead foil, triple bagged and taped. Understood?"

"*Da, da.* Understood. *Paka.* Later, my friend."

I am not your damn friend, Hamadi thought as he turned away without responding.

By the next night, the rain had turned to light snow, and a palette stacked with neat, plastic-wrapped packets waited for Hamadi on the loading platform. Hamadi jumped nimbly out of the panel truck, ran around, and hopped up onto the concrete platform, while his driver, a skinny young man from a mostly Muslim enclave just over the border, finished backing up. The panel truck jolted to a stop just short of the tailboard, and the driver started to step out of the cab. Hamadi took one look at the palette and waved the approaching driver back into the truck. In clumsy Russian he told the two guards standing near the palette to get the goods loaded quickly, before they attracted attention. The guards looked dumbly at each other but otherwise made no move.

"Doesn't Glinkov maintain any discipline?" Hamadi said.

"Ah, English. Better. Discipline? Yes. But we are not stevedores. Load it yourself."

Hamadi looked again at the tiers of nearly identical packets and shook his head. "Glinkov will not be pleased if he learns that we drove off without the shipment. He will want the rest of his fee. And it is not like there are many markets in which to sell goods such as these—at any price. I think you would be wise to load them now." He started back toward the front of the truck. The two men sighed and began heaving the packets casually onto the floor in the back.

Hamadi's driver scowled at him. "What was that about? We could have loaded the stuff."

"Sure, if we wanted to die young, which has never been my plan nor should it be yours. You must attend to small details. There was powder on the outside of some of the packets. They were careless packing the material. Their mistake. Let them pay the penalty."

The driver nodded knowingly as he watched in his rearview mirror.

Too bad for the mules, though, Hamadi thought. But mules are mules, and we are all *jihadi*. Each must contribute as he can.

After they finished loading, one of the guards came around to the open window and held out his hand. "Good luck," he said. Hamadi looked down at the man's hand, rolled up the window, and signaled to his driver to pull out. The guard thrust his middle finger in the air and cursed him loudly in Bulgarian.

Pity, thought Hamadi as they rolled out into the night heading toward the frontier. He pulled out his smartphone and brought up a calendar. The agreed delivery date was creeping up on them quickly, but they would make it to the boats and then get it to the mules who would smuggle it the final leg to where it was needed, where it would be prepared for use, where it would become the Sword of the Prophet. He checked to see that there was enough signal, then expertly thumbed a three-word text message on the numeric pad: 7-666-99 666-66 2-555-555. He sent it, then shut off the phone and swapped out the SIM card for a new one. The old one he snapped in two and tossed out the window into the snow. Track that, he thought.

2

K arl Lustig, a bit winded from the run up the switch-back trail from the beach at Ga'ash, worked to control his breathing. Now, he thought, that is a true sign of getting old. When you start to cover up being out of breath after running uphill, you are on your way downhill. When you cover up and there is no one even around to notice, you are already old. No, he protested in a silent shout. Not old, he mentally chided himself, not yet. *Older* perhaps, as in older Americans, that wonderful euphemism of sociologists and the welfare state of my homeland. Older than who? Older than me. As for me, I for one am sure not ready to hang up my running shoes, no way. With all these new responsibilities coming my way, the word retirement is not even in my vocabulary. I had better stay young. And in shape.

Karl still found his circumstances surprising. After decades of suitcase living and singlehood, he was finally settled down, but neither as nor where he could ever have imagined. A part of him would always see himself as a small-town boy uprooted from the Upper Midwest by college and circumstances. His four years at MIT had forever changed his view of the world, which had almost overnight become so much larger, populated not only with amazing and diverse people, but jammed with wondrous boxes of blinking lights and glowing tubes that did the bidding of anyone with knowledge of the secret languages by which they were commanded. He had been seduced by their flashing indicators and their phosphorescent displays into a career as a computer consultant. And then, on one consulting trip to Germany, his peripatetic but comfortable life had been derailed by a collision with an old friend from MIT, another transplanted mid-westerner who was, it turned out, manipulating strings behind the scene that would ultimately pull Karl to Israel and to a new life—a settled life with a wife and family that would find him progressively less and less of a consultant and ever more of a commentator.

Now, he turned to wave back to his stepson and his wife—his pregnant wife—both still playing on the beach. He looked around for just the right spot on the grassy edge of the cliff from which to sit and watch them as they maneuvered the enormous blue-and-white kite that twisted and turned above the sand and rocks and waves. So beautiful, he thought, so beautiful, both of them. My Shira, my Binyamin. Their long shadows in the late afternoon sun danced across the beach that stretched away below him in both directions. The weather was too cool and windy now for a swim or for sunbathing, and the young gays playing beach volleyball were gone, but with a steady on-shore wind against its dramatic cliffs, Ga'ash was a perfect spot for sailing a kite or for hang-gliding off the cliffs or for sitting and watching the kites and the hang-gliders and the watchers.

It also seemed the perfect place to spend the last day before Karl had to leave for a conference in Boston. He smiled to himself, thinking back to the first time Shira had brought him to Ga'ash beach. They had been playing hooky from work while Bini was in school. On a whim they had turned it into a morning of swimming and sunning and stealing kisses and caresses before hurrying back to the apartment to make love ahead of Bini's return from school. And now Bini was studying for his bar mitzvah. It had been another day, like this one, that he would gladly have stretched from mere hours into languorous days. But Karl, now as then, had responsibilities waiting in Boston. Although he still often referred to Boston as "back home," and usually relished each return visit on business, in his heart, Israel had become his real home, or at least that stretch of it from Haifa down to Tel Aviv that spanned his regular beat as a columnist and a blogger writing on the events and arcana of Israel's whirlwind high-tech world.

Amidst the kites and the hang gliders, Karl noticed another shape, a brilliant yellow cross carving a lazy spiral against the blue and silver of the sky. At first he thought it was a full-sized glider, but then realized it was an exceptionally large radio-controlled model. He looked around for someone holding a little box with joysticks and a jutting antenna, but the only technology in sight was in the hands of an older gentleman sitting in a car across the road with the passenger door propped open, plunking away on a laptop computer.

What a shame, Karl thought, to waste a day such as this sitting in your car answering email or surfing the Web. There was something odd, though, about the man's intermittent two-finger typing and the way he kept crouching over to squint at the laptop screen, then leaning out to check the sky. Tall and distinguished, he sat half in and half out of the tiny gray Fiat that confined him like a cage. He seemed as much interested in something above him as in the computer in his lap. Finally, Karl made the connection: computer control. From the pacing of the actions on the computer, he surmised that the glider must be semi-autonomous, rather than directly controlled, that the man with the laptop was apparently sending it only general commands.

Now that is way cool, Karl thought, smiling and nodding in the direction of the car. For a moment, just a moment, the man paused and looked toward Karl but then turned quickly back to his business with the laptop.

The radio-controlled glider spiraled slowly and seductively skyward on the updraft off the cliffs, drawing the eye and silently calling to the watcher to follow, until, for a moment, it seemed to pause and sit in the air. Without warning, it nose-dived, dragging something behind it. The glider had tangled with the unseen string of a high-flying kite. The man at the laptop tapped madly at the keyboard, but there was nothing that could be done. The once-graceful glider tumbled and cork-screwed awkwardly before crashing onto the rocks at the edge of the shore. Onlookers on the beach rushed to the site of the crash as the man in the car, without hesitating so much as a moment, closed his laptop, extricated himself from his auto-motive cage, and walked briskly around to get into the driver's seat before quickly driving off.

How odd, thought Karl, just as Bini came running up from the beach. "Did you see that, Abba Karl? That was sick! Just awesome! It just went whang and then like this." He demonstrated with his hands. "Did you see it? Awesome. It hit the beach like a bomb. Pfloom. Like a bomb. See, I got a piece of it." He proudly held up a broken circuit board from the radio-control system or the on-board computer. "Is that sick, or what!?"

Bini turned and scrambled back down toward his mother, shouting and waving his souvenir. Shira, her dark hair tousled by the wind, smiled up at Karl. Such love in her eyes, Karl thought.

3

The two young women in their fashionably scuffed jeans talked quietly as they moved slowly with the crowd of the pious and the curious. The heat of the midmorning sun bounced off ancient stone and beat upon them from every quarter. They were immersed in a rich stew of sound, a jumble of languages and agendas, and, at a distance, a potpourri of muffled pleas and prayers.

Clarissa Hargrove, wishing she were not so tall, not so pale, not so glaringly a touring student on break, bent down to her traveling companion and said in a half-whisper, "Tell me again why we are here, Josie? I'm not Jewish. You're not Jewish. So why are we going to the Wailing Wall?" Clarissa had a history of following her friend's lead until they were in the thick of something, at or near the point of no return, only then to start questioning or voicing uncertainty about the virtues of their venture.

Josie pushed back a wayward strand of her mahogany hair and smiled up at her friend. "Who knows," she said, shrugging her shoulders dramatically. "Most Portuguese have some Jewish blood in them, you know." She was Clarissa's physical and emotional opposite: pretty, petite, quick-tempered. The two were joined by bonds of mutual envy, the one wishing she were taller, more elegant, more controlled, the other wanting to be smaller, cuter, more spontaneous.

Clarissa wiggled her shoulders awkwardly, as if shrugging off some uncomfortable piece of clothing. "I thought your family was Spanish. Mexican. What do you Americans say? Hispanic? Latinos?"

"Mafalda José Castanheira Pereira. Portuguese." She said dramatically, pronouncing each syllable with a careful continental accent, rolling her R's and buzzing the soft consonant at the start of her second name. A silent tremor of laughter rippled through her small frame as she finished with a slight curtsy and a nod.

"Mafalda José? What kind of a name is that? I mean, I thought your name was Josie. Isn't José, like, I mean, it sounds like a boy's name?"

"Well, yes, but that's the way it is with the Portuguese. My father's name was José Duarte. His family was from Madeira, see. So I go by Josie because my first name is just too weird, and it's a drag to keep explaining why a girl would have a boy's name. Besides, in the States they always pronounce it wrong when they read it. Ho-say. Yuk. Like if it was Spanish. At least your parents gave you a solidly mainstream name.

Anyway, Pereira is a pretty strong clue. Back in the fifteenth century, when the Portuguese Jews were forced to convert, many took the names of trees for their Christianized surnames. Pereira, pear tree. My mom's maiden name was Castanheira. Chestnut tree. See? Both sides."

"I never knew. And Mafalda? Where is that from, what does that mean?"

"It means my mother was a cruel bitch. Not." She paused for effect. "No, I think it was the name of a Portuguese princess, but I don't know if it means anything. My parents always say it's such a beautiful name. Go figure. Anyway, we are not Jewish, but the family might have been, five centuries back. We are nominally Catholic on both sides, although my dad has never attended Mass, and my mom rejected the papal bullshit when she was just a girl. She said that a loving God would never condemn unbaptized babies to hell or purgatory. Of course, now the Pope has declared there is no purgatory. Popes are imperfect and fallible, my mother would say. They change their minds and contradict themselves and each other, she would add, compounding her blasphemy.

"And you know me. I waffle between atheism and animism, depending on the time of the month. But I still want to leave a prayer in the wall for my great grandmother. I never knew her, but people say I look like her, and the family story, unconfirmed, is that she converted in order to marry into our family. So I asked Tovah—you know, that girl from poli-sci class—to write out a prayer that I could tuck into the wall in her honor. So I guess, nominally, officially, or maybe unofficially, maybe I am. Jewish, that is. A Jewish grandmother, you know, that counts. So great grandmother must be almost as good. And here we are in Jerusalem and on our way to the

Wailing Wall.

"After that, let's go around and up to see the Temple Mount itself and the Dome of the Rock. I understand it is really awesome. Isn't it ironic? Jews were here long before Mohammed launched Islam, but they are left with the rocky ruins of one fragment of their temple while the Muslims have this magnificent mosque right on top. The Jews pray in the ruins below while their Muslim brothers worship in splendor above. If you want to know what I think ..."

She was interrupted by a sound like microwave popcorn just beginning to pop: brief, irregular bursts, sharp but muffled. Josie, standing on tiptoes in the hope of seeing what was happening, faced toward the popping sound, which stopped even as she turned. She listened for a moment, as did others in the crowd, then said, "What was that? Did you hear that?" Clarissa didn't answer, and when Josie turned back, she didn't see her at first. Instead she noticed a small knot of people kneeling around something on the ground.

Harold Timothy was an unlikely archeologist. For one thing, Indiana Jones had spoiled it for the entire profession by so becoming the unconscious archetype in the public mind that almost everyone told Harold he simply did not look the part. Small-boned and soft-spoken, with a perpetually adolescent face, he had often been told that he looked more like a med student on some television daytime drama than like a biblical archeologist. Indeed, he had started out to be a medical missionary, but fortuitously fell under the spell of ancient artifacts in an elective class on biblical archeology while he was still in pre-med at a small Christian college in Arkansas. He had finished his medical degree out of a sense of duty reinforced by the pull of an all-expenses scholarship, then started working at a tiny rural church-run hospital in the Philippines until, on learning in 2001 that missionaries Martin and Gracia Burnham had been abducted from nearby by a group of Abu Sayyaf terrorists, he began to doubt whether he had been truly called. When he learned of Martin Burnham's death in a botched rescue raid, he discovered both the limits of his own faith and courage and the depth of his scholarly passions. He returned to graduate school, started doing field research in the Holy Land, and, drawing on his boyhood experiences spelunking in southern caves, had become a respected leader of subterranean expeditions.

The archeology beneath Jerusalem's Old City was going well. Harold and his students from the Biblical Field Research Center were becoming adept with the little semi-autonomous robots that were now the mainstay of his field work. He had been skeptical at first, after an anonymous donor had sent several of the little tracked vehicles to his department, but they were proving to be a true godsend, enabling his team to study unexplored and once unreachable parts of ancient sewers and cellars without having to launch any major excavation. The robots could squeeze through openings too small for even the slimmest and most agile young archeology student and could enter spaces unsafe for any human being. They could photograph markings on the wall in infrared and ultraviolet as well as in visible light. If they found an interesting artifact, they could scan it *in situ* with a laser to create a computer file that could later be downloaded to a computer-controlled tool in the lab back at the Research Center in Arkansas, producing an exact three-dimensional replica in plastic without ever having touched the original.

The robots did the dirty work while Harold and his two student archeologists sat in air-conditioned comfort in their all-white minivan, studying their screens and maps and working the controls of their robotic assistants. Technology was helping them in their field research, in their analysis, even in sharing the data. Their maps and images and findings were uploaded by satellite link almost as soon as they were available in the mobile control center. An unexpected uptick in generous donations from wealthy conservatives had transformed Harold's lab into a showcase for modern high-tech archeology. He smiled to think of his strictly secular colleagues struggling for meager government grants when he had money and equipment raining down on him, unasked, like manna before the Israelites in the desert.

Robots are so much better than grad students, Harold thought, glancing over to the third robot in the corner, the one they kept as a spare. Like the others, it had an articulated camera head and a double-jointed arm atop a chassis with two pairs of tank-like treads. The chassis could bend on two axes to get over or around most anything. The robot could climb stairs or lower itself by cable into a cistern. It was even rather cute in a mechanical sort of way. Of course, live graduate students had other things to offer in the field, particularly the young Canadian, Gillian Walkenberg, on whom Harold had set his sights from the first time he had interviewed her by video conference. Nothing had happened yet, but the semester was only half over. He was not sure of the depth of her commitment to Christ, but then, he was not sure of his own, either.

"We've lost Shadrach," Chris Barrone, the younger of his two students, said, pointing at one of the screens on the operator console before adding, "again." He pushed back a shock of his shoulder-length blonde hair as he turned to Harold with a pleading expression on his face. Harold grudgingly tolerated the young man's ambiguous sexuality, in part because it meant less competition. Hate the sin, but love the sinner. That was the credo that Harold struggled to live up to and that he hoped would be applied to himself, sinner that he was and sinner that he longed to be.

Harold squeezed past Gillian, savoring the press of her shoulder and the heady scent of her hair, and sat down beside Chris, who was jiggling a joystick and punching buttons in front of an all-blue monitor screen displaying a flashing legend: No Signal, No Signal.

"He disconnected from the umbilical, shifted into local Wi-Fi mode, and started down a side tunnel. Then the feed went blank." Chris twisted a dial and punched a couple of buttons half-heartedly before continuing. "He does this, goes off on his own for a while, then comes back, plugs into the umbilical again, and behaves himself for the rest of the mission. We checked him over and can't find anything wrong with him or with his programs. He just takes off sometimes. Meshach never acts up, at least so far. We've tried to find out what Shadrach does and where he goes when he's off on these little jaunts, but the onboard camera and event recorders also cut off, so we get nothing when we take a dump.

"But you know what really frosts me? Look at that," he said, pointing to a flickering yellow-green light in one corner of the console. "That's disk activity, just as if we were getting a normal feed and the raw data were being written to the hard drive. Except right now there's no feed as far as we can tell, and at the end of the day, we can't find anything in the folder for Shadrach or anywhere else for the time while he is AWOL.

Weird stuff, like poltergeists."

Harold scowled. "No such thing. I'll not have my students blaming imaginary forces or invoking magical thinking to explain what are just technical failures. Nor are such beliefs acceptable to good young Christians. Did you ever try to follow him with Meshach to see what he's up to? That is what a scientist would do."

Duly chastised, Chris went on the defensive. "Easier said than done. It's a stretch to control two of them at once, so we started running only one robot at a time, and by the time we could get Meshach or Abednego booted up and lowered down the well, Shadrach would be back among the living. The times we have used the robots in tandem, Shadrach was as good as gold."

"Well, if this keeps up, let's start running two at once as often as we can. Or don't use Shadrach as the primary. We do have three robots."

"But, Shadrack is bigger. He has the longer arm and the tool changer, plus a much bigger battery for when he's off the umbilical."

"Figure it out," Harold said. "We can't afford to have blanks in the record. Or to lose a robot." He glanced out of the windscreen of the van just in time to catch a glimpse of the red star and flashing light on the back of a *Magen David Adom* motorcycle speeding past on the narrow street. The Red Shield first responders were famous for being quick on the scene, and the motorcycles meant they could get almost anywhere in the Old City.

"Someone must be hurt," he said, as he climbed past Gillian again to squeeze into the front passenger seat. "I'll go check it out." He grabbed the emergency medical kit from under the seat before pushing open the door and starting out at a trot after the motorcycle.

4

Lev Novikov glared at the spinning beach ball floating in the middle of his laptop screen and cursed. His eyes refocused on his own reflection in the glossy screen. Maturely handsome, that was how his friends would describe him. Mature, meaning getting old, is how he would describe himself. His eyes had a steely Slavic intensity inherited from his father, but he had his mother's coarse and unruly hair, which had begun to thin and retreat from the prominent brow line that set off his piercing eyes. He had long thought of his hair color as salt-and-pepper, but even that euphemism was losing its salience, as the peppering of dark strands became lost in a sea of purest salt. He shook his head. So near retirement, he thought, isn't it time you learned some patience? *V'im lo akshav, ematai?* If not now, when, old man? Well, not now, not today. We absolutely must check out that informant now, now before the meeting, before we get into bed with the wrong whore.

The week had started badly and had gone downhill from there. He had thought he'd seen the worst of it after the shooting of an English girl in Jerusalem, but now nothing seemed to be going right, and this was beginning to feel like the norm. Lev wondered whether things in Israel were really any different than in the past or whether it was just his perspective that had changed since becoming desk-bound. He had worked for Mossad, the Institute, most of his adult life, but his last field assignment had been years earlier, following up on the death of his best friend and former Mossad agent, an Israeli-American named Migdal Rozeyn.

Oddly, the more technology interceded between Lev and events on the ground, the more they seemed to impact him emotionally. As a field agent he had been a paragon of calm self-control; as a senior manager he often struggled to keep his emotions in check.

Lev jiggled the mouse, hit the Enter key several times, then hammered away on the Escape key so hard that the laptop almost bounced on his desk. "What the hell is with the system, Shimon?" he yelled out the door. "I can't even get a damned log-in screen." Shimon Weiszkopf, whose office was diagonally across from his, didn't answer.

His always-able but unfailingly anxious assistant, Rahel Hassan, stopped outside his door, her usual look of studied distress magnified into a mask of near panic. "Shimon's down at the farm dealing with some kind of massive attack. Somebody's got a whole bot brigade pounding away at our gateway." Before Lev could do or say anything, she headed down the hall at a trot, her jet-black hair streaming behind her.

A petite woman in her forties who still wore her hair in a girlish ponytail, Rahel reminded Lev of a squirrel—hyper- vigilant, always dodging and darting, pausing then panicking. Her way of moving and of being drove Lev crazy, but she was both very good at what she did and completely lacking in ambition, which made her the perfect assistant. The fact that she seemed to Lev to harbor fantasies of someday becoming Mrs. Novikov only added an extra dimension to her loyalty. By the time she truly understood that neither she nor anyone else was likely ever to become Mrs. Novikov, Lev would be retired. At least so he figured.

Lev put his laptop to sleep, tucked it under his arm, and headed down the hall in the opposite direction. The server farm was not his direct responsibility, but it was his concern, as was almost everything at the moment, or so it seemed to him. He was beginning to wonder why he had ever agreed to a promotion.

Something like this always seemed to happen exactly in the moment of greatest need, he thought, cursing the computers that had become like an essential but often untrustworthy partner in a messy business arrangement. Stepping off the elevator, he surrendered his laptop to the grim-faced guard at the entrance to the sub-basement complex, then negotiated his way through the layers of security: RFID badge, face recognition, fingerprint scan, and finally his personal access code on the keypad next to the last door.

The room, filled with racks upon racks of blinking boxes, was quiet except for the *sotto voce* whine of whirling disk drives and the breathy whistle of the cooling fans. Straight ahead, surrounded by the eager and attentive young geek squad that kept the systems of the server farm humming for the Institute, was Shimon Weiszkopf, standing with his hand over his mouth and shaking his balding head as he stared at a screen full of bouncing red and blue bars and obscure codes scrolling by too fast for the eye to follow. Somehow it all seemed to make some kind of sense to Shimon. He glanced up as Lev crossed toward him.

"They're not getting in, if that's what you're worried about. This is a really massive, sophisticated, and coordinated attack, but the firewall is solid, and there is no real connection between the public site and any of our secure systems, as you well know."

"Then why can't I get a login screen for Gesher Tsar?" Gesher Tsar, or Narrow Bridge, was the code name used for the complex of computers and software that monitored and probed the Web, perpetually churning through millions upon millions of pages and postings in search of patterns that might contain hints of terrorist intentions or might open the trail to a malevolent group or help uncover the truth about a suspect informer. It was Israel's sophisticated homegrown successor to the storied PROMIS system developed by Inslaw in the U.S. in the 1970s and 1980s, and the ECHELON system that the Americans used to track electronic communications worldwide.

"I don't know exactly what's wrong, but it's probably a side effect of having isolated all the inside systems and segmented the network. That and everybody trying at once to find out what's going on. If we can't stop the storm by bouncing traffic, we'll take the public site down, then if that doesn't work, we'll disconnect completely from the outside world. But that would leave field offices and operatives out of contact, so we're escalating by steps." He paused, clearly pleased by his own play on words, then added, "If I can be allowed to use a metaphor mash-up."

"Skip the mash-ups and the metaphors, Shimon; stick with stark reality. Just do it. If I can't even access the system from here, do you think anyone in Haifa can? The field offices are already on their own. Cut the cord. Now."

"Yeah, right. Okay." Shimon huffed loudly as he typed his way through a series of screens, got a prominent flashing warning message, then simultaneously pressed four keys to confirm the command. "There, we're in bunker mode. Nothing digital gets in or out. Only the offices with high security nodes and computers equipped with the special issue network cards being operated from inside this building even work. I assume that's you."

"I assume. Got an Ethernet cable, so I can check? I'll go grab my laptop."

"You can't do it in here. Security reasons, you understand. There are no open Ethernet jacks in the entire room. Not even a USB port."

"Well, then I'm back to my office. Get this sorted out immediately, and I do mean immediately. And, of course, there's a lid on this. Make sure all your techies understand that none of this is for discussion anywhere, anytime, or with anyone. Period. Understood?"

"Look, my people are professionals, just like yours. Every one of them has been vetted for the highest clearance. They know the rules."

"Of course they do, but I also know how easily these technical types get into heated discussions in on-line forums or launch technical debates with colleagues at a conference on supposedly abstract topics or hypothetical scenarios. From the abstract and hypothetical to conjecture and to confirmation is such a short stroll, particularly for this country's journalists. Even if we manage to put the lid on things at home, the foreign press would have a field day. This business will get into the media somehow whatever we do, and it will be bad enough. I just don't want any unmanaged discourse, not even a single word of it. So remind everybody. Tell them it comes from the top. And stop into my office when you've got this mess under control."

"You're the boss," Shimon responded, with only the faintest note of sarcasm.

Lev smiled. "That I am. At least as far as you are concerned." In practice, he and Shimon got along well enough, but Shimon had always resented being passed over for Lev's position. Of course, it had been no accident. Shimon was a gifted conductor when it came to orchestrating the technology, while Lev was the instrumentalist who excelled at coordinating the people. Shimon, however, looked on the whole affair as nepotism; Lev's father had been near the top at the Institute and had shepherded the careers of both his son and his son's best friend, Migdal Rozeyn, the young American who had come to be treated like family and who had actually led the way into the intelligence services even before Lev followed in his father's footsteps.

It had taken Lev until long after his compulsory army service to get past his need to rebel against a domineering father who incessantly extolled the virtues of Israeli intelligence, although he never spoke a word about his own role. In a twist of sibling irony, Migdal, the unofficially "adopted" son from America, had expressed his own rebellion against a country that he felt had long ago abandoned him, by converting to Judaism, becoming an Israeli citizen, and joining Mossad.

Back in his office, Lev paused at the door with its discreet sign in English and Hebrew: Chief of Technical Services. The Technical Services Department was one wave in a steady sea-change within the Institute as well as a new chapter in Lev Novikov's career. The backbone and sinew of Mossad and the source of its well-deserved reputation as one of the world's most elite intelligence service had long been its reliance on HUMINT, human intelligence, the product of competent and persistent people on the ground using their eyes and ears and wiles to gather and interpret information of value. The Institute, or at least its old-guard traditionalists, sneered at larger and better-funded services, like the American CIA and NSA or Great Britain's MI5 and MI6, that increasingly preferred to invest their faith—and their money—in satellite reconnaissance and electronic eavesdropping and computerized tracking of emails, all the myriad manner of glitzy technology known in the trade by the archaic term of SIGINT: signal intelligence. Lev was among the ambivalent many who, even as they surfed the waves of change, were not yet completely comfortable with the shifting priorities and responsibilities as SIGINT moved from a supporting role toward featured performance at center stage.

How far you've come, he chided himself. Or how low you have sunk. You were a *katsa*. You and Migdal were field agents fighting the enemies of Israel around the world, and now you are a damned desk-warming do-nothing poring over your charts and reports and spreadsheets, fighting uncooperative networks and inadequate software, chasing digital terrorists in cyberspace with your fingers instead of in the world on your own two feet.

What would Migdal think? He would have laughed and said "Nothing lasts." He had been fond of quoting Sheldon Kopp, an American self-help author that he was forever urging Lev to study. Kopp may not have been a sage in the mold of Hillel the Elder, Lev mused, but he succinctly nailed that particular one. Nothing lasts. Nothing. Lev made a mental note to dig up the paperback book Migdal had given him so many years ago, not long after they had started to work together. What a title, Lev thought. *If You Meet the Buddha on the Road, Kill Him.* So many dead Buddhas, so little insight. Will the human race ever grow up? Probably not any time soon, he thought. Lev had always intended to read the book but had never gotten around to it, like so many of the personal things on his must-do list, a list that had always been edged out by work.

Lev sat down at his desk, reconnected his laptop, and, on the third try, was finally able to log-in to Gesher Tsar. With access to the outside world cut off, though, he was limited in what he could do, so he abandoned his online pursuit of information about the informant and instead pulled up some day-old reports that he had intended to study more closely. Some of the bright boys down the hall had been monitoring an obscure website used as a drop box and disguised discussion forum by an ill-defined mix of misfits with little in common beyond their shared anti-Israeli sentiments. Chatter on the Internet had begun to hint that something was going on, something possibly being coordinated or instigated through this site. In particular, offhand references to Al Aqsa had been rising for weeks. After hacking into the site, Mossad had begun backtracking the Internet addresses of visitors and posters.

Not surprisingly, many trails ended at public libraries or cybercafés, but some pointed back at particular subscribers to regular services.

A map display of the Internet addresses showed dense blobs of red in several areas around the globe, but Lev's eye was drawn to a few isolated dots in Israel. He zoomed in, resolved the display into a scattering of locations in Tel Aviv and Haifa, then clicked to correlate the IP addresses with provider databases and other resources, to see if he could resolve any of them to individual accounts. He scrolled quickly down the list of names and addresses, then stopped and backed up. He sucked in his breath suddenly as he recognized the name of a subscriber in Haifa.

"What the fuck are you up to, Karl Lustig?" he said to the display. "I think we better have a talk." He switched to his personal contact list and reached for his unsecured phone just as Shimon poked his head into the office.

"It stopped," Shimon said. "The attack just stopped. The backdoor probes just stopped. I am beginning to think it might have been just an exercise, a test of some kind, but I don't see the point. They never got in, they never got anything, they never hurt us. We closed down before they could get anywhere."

"Maybe they never intended to get in. Perhaps we did just what they wanted us to, and once they were satisfied, they backed off."

Shimon scrunched up his face in puzzled concentration for several seconds, then turned and left without saying anything more.

Lev stared at the empty doorway. The borders that we must patrol just keep growing, he thought, even as the land seems to shrink. And the enemies multiply, as do the so-called friends who fight us more than they defend us. He leaned back in his chair as far as he could and closed the door to his office before picking up his phone again and dialing a number in Haifa.

The message, hidden in plain sight, as it were, was simple and direct. "Operation Trebuchet went as planned. It will work again when needed. For delivery, we're chipping away on a breakthrough. All will be ready." There was another message, a single word, broadcast for all the world to see, had they only eyes with which to see it and brains with which to understand. "Pox," it said.

5

Karl Lustig charged into the gray concrete fortress of Boston's Hines Convention Center through the Boylston Street entrance, flashed his conference badge to the sleepy security guard, and headed down the dark corridor at a near trot toward the escalators. The signage for the Internet Journalism Congress was not very good, but the Hines was Karl's old stamping grounds, and he had already scoped out the rooms the night before when he had checked in to pick up his conference material.

He was not late, not yet, but his session on "The Journey from Journalism to Journals: Writing for Alternate Audiences" had been relegated to one of the smaller breakout rooms on the third floor, at the far end of the corridor, and he wanted to have time for a test run on the audio-visual equipment.

Oversleeping was not standard procedure for Karl, whose punctuality was legendary among his colleagues and clients, but he was still jet-lagged from the flight from Zurich where potential consulting clients had run him ragged over a day and a half of non-stop demos and dinners. And he was anticipating with some ambivalence getting on a plane headed back to Israel at the end of the day. It would be a long flight made longer still by crying babies at the back and devout Jews praying in the aisles and an economy seat that would only recline a few inches.

Karl had thought he was being clever to pack several objectives into one trip, but the result was a zig-zag itinerary chopped into too many long hauls and short nights. The alternative would have meant being away from home longer, which he wanted to avoid, considering Shira's condition and all. He now realized that he should never have submitted a session proposal to the IJC this year. But, then, he thought, I always take on too much, don't I. "You'd think I would learn one of these years," he said aloud to no one in particular.

At the series of escalators, Karl took the steps two at a time, then speed-walked toward the room at the end of the hall. Karl hated the Hines, and made no apologies for referring to it as a modern monstrosity. He regarded it as one of the ugliest convention facilities on the planet: dark, gray, cold, and imposing, like New England winter at its worst. It was a vast and inefficient space, with nothing within designed to a human scale.

When he reached the windowless room to which he had been assigned, the very last along the hall, it was empty except for a young woman with purple hair standing inside the door and holding a stack of paper. His student volunteer, he guessed.

"Hi, I'm Candy McGeorge," she said. "I'm in the digital arts program at BU. I'll be helping you with your session today. I can't tell you how much I admire your writing. I had to trade with one of my buds to get your session."

Karl smiled skeptically. I'll bet you did, he thought. And after your friend took the session you really wanted you quickly crammed on my columns just in case I asked you about them—which I won't. "Well, that's wonderful, Candy," he said aloud. "You can most help now by seeing if you can find someone from audio-visual. There was supposed to be a projector in here. And a wireless mike."

"Oh, right. I'll, like, just go," she said, flipping a hand toward the door and following it as if being led away by some invisible abductor.

Karl smiled again. Good, you just do that, he thought. As long as you get my projector and microphone and keep from getting underfoot, I'll be happy as a Cape Ann clam. He headed for the front of the room, climbed up on the riser, and started rearranging the podium, table, and chairs to make it easier to walk around, interact with the audience, and still show his PowerPoint slides.

Five minutes before the scheduled start of the session, a few people finally drifted in and sat in awkward silence toward the back, scanning the room self-consciously and checking their programs as if assessing whether they were in the right place or trying to make up their minds about leaving for another, better attended session. There was still no sign of the purple-haired volunteer or the audio-visual people. Karl was about to go out in search of one or both when his cellphone buzzed against his hip. Karl grabbed it, hoping it was not from home, which could only mean a crisis of one sort or another. The caller ID was unknown, maybe out-of-country, so he flipped the phone open anxiously.

"Yeah? Karl Lustig here."

"Karl, it's Lev, Lev Novikov. Shira gave me your cell number and said you were in the U.S. I hope I haven't called at a bad time. It's early morning there, right? So how are you, anyway?"

"Well, wow. I am fine. Talk about a voice from the past. What's up? What's the occasion for a personal call from a highly placed source in the Israeli intelligence community? And how are you?"

"Not so highly placed, to be truthful. Which is more candor than you'll get out of most of my brethren here. I called because I just wanted to see you and Shira and talk with you. I know you get in late tomorrow, but I wondered if you might be up for having an old friend for dinner. Shira says it's all right with her if it's okay with you."

"You sound like our son when he's after something and is attempting to play us off against each other. But, yeah, I suppose. I'm not sure I will be that good as company right after flying six thousand miles. I don't get into Tel Aviv until two something in the afternoon."

"I hear what you're saying, but it would be good if we could talk again, face-to-face. It's not something I would discuss over the phone."

Karl recognized the serious overtones in Lev's voice. He had come to know that voice all too well when they had briefly worked together. "You can't give me a hint?" he said.

Lev said nothing for a couple of seconds, then, "Look, if it's too much to ask of the returning road warrior eager to have time with his family, we can put it off another day. But it would be great if you could."

That clinched it for Karl, who could tell that there was not really any option. "All right, Lev," he said. "It will be good to catch up. Look, I gotta go. The long lost A/V guy has finally materialized with my projector, and I have a conference presentation scheduled to start," he looked at his watch, "three minutes ago. So, Thursday night, then. *L'hitraot.*"

"Shalom, Karl."

As the A/V technician focused and adjusted the projector, Karl looked out over the audience of grim faces and bored expressions scattered throughout the room and knew he was in for a challenge. You're a pro, he told himself, rise to the occasion.

After a late start with a balky mike that Karl finally gave up on and turned off, the ninety-minute session dragged. Karl gave it his best, but getting audience participation from the dozen people who stuck it out to the bitter end was like digging dandelions out of the cracks between pavers in a garden walkway. By the time the last of the attendees drifted out, Karl was so discouraged that he decided to blow off the afternoon sessions. He packed up his laptop and laser pointer to head back to his place on Beacon Hill.

Keeping his old apartment for such occasional trips to Boston was a guilty luxury, but Shira had always insisted that it was a legitimate business expense. It was actually paid for by Benjamin and Hamm LLC, the real-estate business started by her late husband and now run by Karl. Although the apartment gave Karl a familiar place to park when back in the States, it was beginning to feel less and less like a comfort zone to him. His roots were now completely entangled with Shira's and tapped deep into the soil of Israel.

At the apartment, he started gathering and organizing his things, repacking for the trip home, and readying the apartment for another several months of abandonment, a routine that he followed rigidly on every trip. Once everything was in the right compartment of his carry-on or the proper pocket in his laptop bag, he poured himself a mug full of the last of the cold coffee, shoved it in the microwave for 88 seconds, then topped it off with milk before pouring the rest of the carton down the drain and stuffing the few assorted perishables into a big green trash bag that he placed by the door so he wouldn't forget it on his way out. He set the coffee on the floor beside the trash, pulled a sticky note from his pocket, scribbled a reminder to himself to pick up a Red Sox cap for Bini at the airport, then stuck it on the door just above the door handle. He retrieved his coffee and took a quick look around to reassure himself that all was in its proper place, then returned to the living room for a few minutes of feet-up time before closing up and heading for the airport.

As he leaned back on the leather couch and slowly sipped his coffee, he began thinking about Lev's call. Lev had always had a certain flare for the dramatic. Years before he had arrived at the very same apartment under false colors, supposedly to return Karl's stolen driver's license.

At the time, Karl thought, none of us knew quite how much we were caught up in the machinery set in motion by that pilfered license. And now, Lev, what machinations are you involved in? What are you going to drag me into this time? What have I done?

6

K arl and Shira's modest second-floor apartment in Haifa seemed pleasantly crowded to Lev. The plain white walls were peppered with black-and-white photographs—macro close-ups of some of Shira's jewelry designs—and the couple's *ketubah*, their wedding contract, hand-painted in bright colors, hung over the sofa. Everywhere were the carefully arranged artifacts and detritus of work and life: stacks of papers, a cellphone, several school books, an unopened package neatly squared with the books. Lev, who had always preferred to see and feel the boundaries of his world, needed visual, physical anchors against the tidal forces of his work, the uncertainties, the imponderables, the endless abstractions which he daily had to navigate.

Shira, making comments about the limits of modern feminism and the importance of male bonding, had already excused herself to tidy up in the adjacent kitchen, leaving Lev and Karl to finish their wine in the sitting room. Bini took advantage of the captive audience by pacing back and forth in front of them, waving his new Boston Red Sox baseball cap as he explained, in excruciating detail, a computer programming problem he was working on and then, without so much as a pause for breath, moved on to telling of the latest in his online finds, an obscure website operated by an American group mapping the underground caverns and cellars and ancient tunnels beneath Jerusalem.

"This is so sweet. They use robots. These little things on treads can crawl around through tunnels and climb over rubble and take pictures and they keep track of their position, so they are building up a map and 3D images and models of stuff they find and ... So, archeologists are doing real science, right here, underneath the Old City."

"What's the group?" Karl asked.

"The Ark-something Biblical something Center for Field Research, something like that. Like I said, they are doing a scientific study of ..."

"I wouldn't call what they do scientific. These so-called biblical archeologists almost always have an agenda. The Christian Bible colleges are the worst. They are always out to prove something, looking for whatever fits their story and ignoring whatever doesn't."

"Who cares, Abba. The stuff is sick, mega sick. You should see the maps and the 3D digital renderings and the false-color photos. I found all these great files down in a directory structure on the site. I don't think they're supposed to be available to the public, but there's no password or anything. So, like, I figured, okay. Want to see them? You can do this, like, virtual fly-through tour through some parts of the tunnels."

"I don't think so, son. Not tonight." Karl looked at his watch. "Don't you have homework?"

"Well, yeah. But ..."

"But then you need to get to it."

Bini rolled his eyes, slapped on his baseball cap, and headed for his room. Lev craned his neck to watch the boy disappear around the corner into his bedroom.

"Bini has really grown," Lev said. "He reminds me so much of his father. He has that solid, ready-to-spring build that I remember in Migdal. Of course, I can also see your influence. On his interests, I mean. He seems to be a very tech-savvy young man. And growing up so fast. Will there be a bar mitzvah soon?"

"Next year," Karl said, as he absent-mindedly straightened the magazines on the coffee table. Karl and the clutter and chaos that was modern Israel were locked in perpetual combat. It was a complete mismatch. But Lev knew Karl's match was not with the country but with the woman. Shira and Karl were *bashert*, fated to be together. Lev envied them and had more than once said so. He was still looking, forever looking, despairing that he might never find a partner for the years that remained.

"And I should warn you," Karl continued, "that he insists his name is Binyamin. When I was about his age I started insisting that my name was Karlfred, which it really was, believe it or not. So I suppose I should have expected this, but he will always be just Bini to me. Of course, he is still too polite to say anything to you, so you can probably get by with almost any form of address. As for me, when I went off to college, to M.I.T, which at the time seemed to me to be another planet in a galaxy far from Michigan, I changed it back, first to Karl and then to KL, in order to sound more hip. Which shows you how long ago I went to school. Hip was before cool, which was before wicked and now sick."

"Sick. That means good, right? Hard to keep up with American slang. It spreads like a virus over the Internet." He smiled, swirled the wine in his glass for a moment, then continued. "Speaking of spreading news, I understand you and Shira may have some. Am I right? Or is this just a rumor among the gossips of the 'Net neighborhood."

"No, it's true. Shira is pregnant," Karl said, nodding thoughtfully.

"Mazel tov!" Lev said, lifting his glass. "I must say, I am impressed that you would take on the role of new father again. Not sure whether it's brave or foolhardy. Or both. You and I are not getting any younger. And Shira is pretty gutsy, too, to become a mother once more." He didn't say "at her age," but it was implied.

"For sure," Karl replied, reflexively lapsing into Upper-Midwest Americanism, which he tended to do whenever he didn't know what to say. My god, he thought, what am I doing? I'm in my sixties, my hair is white, and I'm an expectant father—for the first time. What a kick in the kiester.

He knew he should say something next. That was the order of polite conversation, and few things ranked higher than order in Karl's personal pantheon, but he was already adrift far from the here-and-now, mentally lost in the enormity of an unfamiliar future, a future drama that featured a new baby at center stage.

Lev interrupted Karl's reverie. "And what does Bini, or Binyamin, think of this?"

"Good question. The very thought that his parents might be doing the nasty turns his stomach. Exact quote. But I think he actually likes babies, although he never admits it. He'll be fine. And is that why you phoned me in America in the middle of my brilliantly boring conference session, invited yourself to dinner, and drove up here after several years? To confirm a rumor?"

"No." He set his glass down. "And I'm sorry if I interrupted something at the conference. No, I have some ... some business to discuss, which is why I waited until we were alone. I shouldn't really even be here, much less talking with you about this business. It is strictly against protocol. But. Bini's father was a dear friend, and I feel obligated to Shira. And to you, of course," he added quickly. "I've never forgotten what you did in Boston."

"Yeah, well neither have I. I still have that Glock that my German friend gave me, by the way, although I haven't touched it since," Karl said, staring into his glass of wine and remembering. "We were lucky, all of us. You don't owe me anything. My only regret," he paused in thought again, "was that nobody stopped the bastard earlier, before he got to Migdal. But then Shira would still be married to Migdal, and she and I would never have met. So maybe things do have a way of working out."

He looked Lev in the eye. "Well then, don't be mysterious about it. Let me guess. You want my help as a security consultant. I read about the bot assault on your computers. It was headline stuff in the American press. Pretty embarrassing, that."

"No, not that. The so-called attack was really just a short-term nuisance. If anything, it gave us a chance to run through our drills and improve our defenses. The hackers may be able to crack into the Pentagon computers, but not ours." He never missed a chance to poke fun at the Americans.

"No, this is another matter. Your name, or more correctly the IP address of your computer, showed up on a terrorist-connected system we have been monitoring. Unless you're working on a story that is rather outside your usual technology beat, it looks pretty hard to explain. Or maybe you have gotten inspired to indulge in some amateur espionage again. I would have thought you had had your fill of that and had settled down into domestic lassitude."

There was one of those meaningful pauses where thoughts are so transparent that nobody speaks them. They were both thinking of Migdal. If it had been Fate that brought Shira and Karl together, then Fate's first name was Migdal.

Lev cleared his throat. "Anyway, I thought I should hear your story first, before the whole Institute starts breathing down your neck and asking a lot of nasty questions."

"I've got nothing to hide. What's the site?" Lev told him. "Never heard of it. Sounds like a social networking site, or maybe a rinky-dink photo sharing operation. You can check my browser history if you want. It's permanent, and I never touch it. It's a tech journalist's audit trail."

"But Karl, the account's got your name on it. How do you explain that?"

"Then it's not me." He turned toward the bedroom and called out, "Adam Binyamin Markham, I need to speak with you. Now."

"What do you mean that it's not you?" Lev asked.

"I work all over the place, so I am on Wi-Fi with an account paid for by InterMetroGroup, publishers of the high-tech rag I do most of my writing for. Shira piggybacks on that for the accounting and website maintenance for her jewelry business. It's an arrangement I have with my editor," he added in a defensive reflex. "The wireless router signal just barely reaches down to her workshop on the ground floor. The only computer on an account that's under my name is Migdal's antique, the laptop that Bini inherited and now has in his bedroom—for his homework, supposedly."

Bini entered the room with a mixture of preadolescent annoyance and anxious anticipation on his face. "Like, what is it? I am trying to finish my algebra homework, you know." He struck an impatient pose just short of insolence. "So?"

Karl put on his best I'm-serious face. "Bini, do you know anything about a website called FaceFolder.org?"

Bini frowned and looked skyward, trying to give the impression he was really puzzling over it, as if trying hard to remember. But Bini had not inherited his father's gift for deception, and neither Lev nor Karl was fooled.

"Bini, this is serious stuff. Talk straight with me. Whatever you've been up to, we're going to find out as soon as we start going through your computer."

Bini took a step back. "No, Dad, no. You don't have to do that. Please. You don't need to look through my computer. I'll tell you."

Lev gave Karl a quick glance, a neutral but knowing look that still said a great deal. They were both remembering what it was like to be twelve.

"Look, son, I'm sure you have private things on there. That's not what this is about. It's about this site. The address of your computer was in its logs. The site is—can I tell him, Lev?—it's run by bad guys."

"I know," Bini said.

Karl glanced again at Lev. "You do?" he said to Bini.

"Well, yeah. See we have this group of kids, a kind of geek squad. We … we hack into webservers and stuff. Look, it's not like we really do anything wrong. It's like spying on the neighbors, seeing what we can discover about who really is who and what they are up to. Like," he started bouncing with excitement, "when that webhosting service in California was taken down last year for spamming. Remember? Well, we were onto them more than a year earlier. We even had billing addresses for some of the Russian and Brazilian mafia who were using the gateway. We even got a Trojan into some of their computers so we could turn the flow of spam on and off. We even—"

"Slow down, Bini, slow down. Are you saying you and your net buddies are, like, amateur cyber-spies or something?"

"Well, yeah. Duh. That's what I was saying. We even …"

Lev laughed. "You are your father's son, that's certain. In a few years we might have a job for you at the Institute."

"Okay, okay, so don't get his hopes up, Lev. Bini, what about FaceFolder.org? What have you been up to with them?"

"That's an interesting case," he said, stroking his chin in a gesture that made Lev almost laugh. "We got onto them from a chain of links that started with ISRA. That's the Indian space program. Hacking into their system was a piece of cake. We eventually got into some computers connected with their atomic research, which led indirectly to Pakistan and then to the Bulgarians and Ukrainians who are trying to peddle a bunch of radioactive stuff."

Lev shook his head, grinning. "Maybe we have a job for

you right now. If you kids have done what you say you have, you may even be a step ahead of us on some fronts. But, back to FaceFolder.org. What do you know about them?"

"All we know is that some of the people who we figured out are, like, maybe trying to buy and sell nuclear stuff, well, they regularly log in there and some have VPN access. You know what that is? Virtual Private Network, like direct connection over the Internet? Yeah, well. Since we already knew other places they visit, we found one that was easy to hack into, planted a drive-by download trap for them to pick up a Trojan that eventually got passed onto FaceFolder.org when they logged in there. We just waited for ET to phone home, and now they are pwned."

"Poned?" Lev asked.

"That's gamer geek-speak for 'owned,'" Karl interjected. "It's spelled p-w-n-e-d. There's an explanation, but don't ask." Lev nodded several times, as if saying that he already knew what the word meant.

"Yeah, right," Bini continued. "We have complete access. In and out whenever we want. We just don't know for sure yet exactly what they're up to, but it's very sneaky stuff, we think. Do you know that a lot of the photos on the site are stock shots? Bogus. Who do they think they are fooling, anyway?"

"Not you and your friends, obviously. Pretty impressive sleuthing," Lev said.

Karl nodded in agreement. "Nothing like a bunch of overly smart teens and preteens with too much time on their hands, right? But, if you guys had full remote access, Bini, why didn't you think to wipe your tracks off the logs."

"My bad," Bini said. "I keep meaning to set up a script

that will do that automatically, but all this homework has really been cutting into my time with the group."

"Don't you have that backwards, son?" Karl said.

"Come on, Abba Karl, do you really think algebra is more important than what we do on TechNahal?"

Karl smiled. "Is that the name of your group, TechNahal?" Bini nodded. It was a play on words, or on acronyms. *Nahal* referred to a youth brigade during Israel's struggle for independence. "So, you are 'fighting pioneer youth' of the Internet, eh? I am pleased to see that you know your country's history. Unfortunately, I think we're going to have to squelch your little hobby. Now, back to your algebra homework, which really is more important than getting in over your head playing spies and counterspies on the Internet."

Bini scowled but turned to leave.

"Not so fast, kid," Lev said, reaching out an arm and hooking it around Bini's waist to stop him. "This is really important stuff. It's absolutely, absolutely essential that you say nothing of this to your friends. Not a word to anybody. No one. This has to be our little secret. Do you understand? We have to be able to depend on you not to compromise our operation. I want you to promise you will not say or send a single word about any of this to anyone. Promise?"

Bini nodded.

"No, say it: I promise not to tell anyone anything about Mossad. Say it."

Bini repeated the words.

"Okay, you can go back to your algebra, Bini."

"Your algebra," Karl added, "Do you hear? No surfing or instant messaging with your spy friends." He gave Bini a gentle shove toward the bedroom.

"Yes, Abba Karl, I hear," he said over his shoulder as he closed the door.

Lev and Karl looked at each other for several seconds. "Do you think he'll keep quiet?" Lev asked.

"I think so. If anything, I believe he takes this whole business of Israeli security too seriously. He knows about his father, of course. It's in his blood, I suppose. So, no, I don't think he'll say anything, but that doesn't mean he'll stay away from his friends or from hacking that website."

"That's okay." Lev reached into his jacket pocket and then held up what looked a bit like a pack of gum. "There's a logger program on this flash drive. As soon as you get a chance, stick it in a USB slot on Bini's computer. The software installs itself. Then we'll be able to follow everything he does. Who knows, he and his whiz-kid friends may find something useful that we miss." He noticed Karl's expression. "I know, I know, you probably don't feel comfortable about spying on Bini, but it's not like you're being a hovering, over-anxious parent. It's national security."

"National security. A lot of questionable stuff gets rationalized in the name of national security. But don't worry, I'll install it. Will you keep me posted if anything I should know about comes up? I mean about Bini's security, not national security. I'm not asking about confidential matters, just about my own kid."

Lev nodded gravely. "I'll let you know if we get anything you should know about." He smiled at Karl. "I must say, you and Shira seem to be doing all right by Bini. It's not easy raising a son these days. Not that I would have firsthand knowledge, but I do have ears and eyes, and I do read the pop sociology stuff in the papers."

Shira, just returning from the kitchen, asked, "What was that all about?"

Lev smiled up at her. She was, if anything, prettier than the young woman that he and Migdal had first met so many years ago, long before Karl had been drawn into their lives. The ringlets of her dark hair were now highlighted with silver, she had that obvious but indefinable glow that some women get in early pregnancy, and her eyes fairly sparkled when she smiled back. I do see what Migdal saw in you, he thought, and how Karl would succumb as well. You are a force, Shira Markham, a beautiful, intelligent, irresistible force. His grin broadened involuntarily.

"What?" she said, giving him a quizzical look.

"Nothing. Nothing really. We were just talking about Bini and this group of adolescent detectives he's involved with, making sure that whatever they find gets passed on to me."

Her mouth opened as her brow knit with disapproval. "What are you saying? You are using Bini to spy on somebody for you? No way. I lost Migdal to you and your almighty Institute and your damn grownup spy games. There is no way you are going to drag my son into that ... that world of yours. He's twelve years old, Lev, twelve. You must be nuts."

Karl crossed over and put a calming hand on her shoulder, which she shrugged off. "It's not what you think. Bini and some online friends have been hacking into computers, one of which just happened to be under scrutiny by Lev's people. Lev is just going to be tracking what Bini does on the Internet, seeing what he learns about a site that's currently being monitored by the Institute."

"And that is supposed to make me feel better? No way. I will not let Bini do it."

"Then we'll have to forbid him to contact his buddies. And I don't believe we would be able to make that stick. He has access to computers at school, too."

"No! I said no."

"What do you think Migdal would have wanted for Bini right now?"

"Don't start with that. We have no idea what Migdal would or would not have wanted. Besides, you and I are raising Bini. And we are not raising him to follow in his father's footsteps. His father's steps led him right into a bullet in the brain, remember. Just because you once got to play cowboy, too, doesn't mean it's okay for our son to play."

Karl held her gaze. "You're right. I'm sorry." He had long ago learned that confrontation was a formula for failure with Shira; complete capitulation was often the shortest route to compromise.

She looked down at him as she chewed on her lip. "All right, all right," she said. "He can keep up with his games, but if anything—anything—happens to him, I'm going to hold you both responsible."

Karl suppressed any reaction to what was so obviously a sincere yet meaningless threat, but Lev spoke up. "I understand. Don't worry, nothing is going to happen." He turned to Karl. "I'm going to list you as a special informant. Bini, too. But don't tell him; we don't want it to go to his head."

Shira threw up her hands as she returned to the kitchen.

Karl scowled. "Is that now Mossad policy? To hire kids. I seem to recall that Migdal, when he arrived in Israel and first got mixed up with you guys, was a lot older than Bini is now. Still, he was put on hold for some years before he was allowed to actually join the team."

"It's just a formality, Karl, but it makes you our assets, which will stop anyone else from poking in and giving you grief, like the spooks from Shin Bet, for instance," he said, referring to Israel's domestic intelligence agency. "Plus, we always have to have all the dots and crosses in place against some misguided oversight group from the Knesset. But," he said, looking at his watch. "I need to get back to Tel Aviv for a day full of meetings tomorrow. I'll say goodbye to Shira and be off."

In the kitchen, he came up behind Shira and placed both hands on her shoulders. "How are your parents? Are they still happy in England, or do you think they might be persuaded to move here to retire?"

Shira pivoted into him and smiled sadly. "Father—may his memory be a blessing—passed away last year. Mum has sold the place in Sheffield and, to the surprise of many, moved back to America. Florida, would you believe? Of course, the fact that my older brother and his husband live there has nothing to do with it, you understand. He was always her favorite. But she does visit us often. In fact, she's planning to spend Passover here with us."

"I am sorry to hear about your father. I have not had much contact with most of my own many scattered cousins. I'm afraid I've been rather buried in work for the last several years, which is an explanation although not an excuse for neglecting you and Bini. And Karl."

"And Karl," she repeated in perfect mimicry, then held up her hand. "No need to apologize. He's an afterthought with my family, too. In a strange way, Mum is more comfortable with her son's husband than with mine. Whenever she talks about Barry and Simon, she manages to work in some comment about Simon being Jewish, too, as if I might forget. Of course, it is really a comment about Karl. Bad enough that I would marry an older man—another older man, my mother would say, as if fingering a fatal character flaw in her daughter—but that he would be a goy … well, there is simply no excuse. Better gay than goy, by her book. Of course, she also opposed my marrying Migdal, not only an older man but a gentile as well. She never took his conversion seriously. Not until now. On almost every telephone call she manages to work in some reference to how impressed she was that Migdal converted, and though she never says it, the implication is clear. Why hasn't Karl converted?"

"Does she realize how cynical Migdal's conversion was? It was an act of personal politics, not some kind of religious rebirth. He was, to his last breath, I am quite sure, a fundamentalist non-believer. He was such a consummate natural actor, though. The Rabbi who tutored him and the Beit Din that examined him were completely taken in, that much is certain."

Shira reached up to place her hand on his shoulder. "Of course, she knows. We all knew. It was more about a stamp on his passport than about God or the *mitzvot* or *halacha*. It was a matter of the laws of Israel rather than the laws of Moses. Migdal was simply not a half-way kind of guy. He wanted to be a full-fledged Jew in a Jewish country. Karl is every bit as committed as Migdal was, he just has no interest in officially joining the tribe. In his heart, I do believe he is coming to think of himself as Jewish, or at least Israeli, and ironically, he is, in his own idiosyncratic manner, more observant than Migdal ever was."

"Yeah, we know. Given the circumstances of losing one of

our top agents and Karl's connection to that whole business, you should not be surprised that we have kept an eye on him. And you. We know that Karl is every bit as straight up as Migdal was devious. Naturally, Migdal's skillful deceptions served our ends well. And maneuvered Karl into your life. Don't forget that."

He bent to kiss her forehead. "I'll go now. Remember that we keep watch. Don't worry about Bini."

"You might as well tell the sun to stop in its tracks. Worry comes with the job for us mothers. And I have added cause for worry, as you well know. They got into this apartment once, and they could do it again, I'm sure. So do keep watch. Do that. But remember that I keep watch as well. *Laila tov*, old friend."

7

He was Adam Binyamin Markham because his father, Migdal Rozeyn, cared nothing for his own invented surname and had wanted to honor Shira's father, Saul Markham, by allowing the Markham family name to continue. But Bini was Migdal's son, with Migdal's stocky build and Migdal's cockiness and intelligence and Migdal's unceasing half-smile. Bini could remember his father, particularly for his wild stories of adventure and intrigue but also for his trips that seemed to his young son to stretch on without end. In a way that Bini would not have been able to explain, his father had almost become more real, more present, since his death, which had so changed his life and his mother's and Karl's. But it was Karl who had bravely stepped into Bini's life after being precipitously drawn into Shira's, whose stories were goofy rather than exciting, who now taught Bini about computers and satellites and lasers more than about good guys and bad guys. Sometimes he was still Abba Karl, a form of address Bini had invented in the early years when his own father was still a vivid memory, but increasingly Karl had become simply Abba, father, the only one Bini really knew. Over the years it had become harder for Bini to picture Migdal's face without confusing it with Karl's. Every so often, he would need to refresh the image in his mind by digging out the picture from the top drawer of his mother's dresser, where it was kept, ever just out of sight yet always ready at hand.

His mother, who had been so many things to him in his short life—shield, confidant, comfort, magician—went by many names. When they spoke in Hebrew, she was still Ima. In English, she was Mom or Mum, depending on whether their conversation of the moment seemed more from the American in her or the British. And on occasion, when he was feeling particularly experimental or bold or grownup, he would call her Shira, upon which she would narrow her eyes in unspoken disapproval but would make no comment.

Bini toggled the screen as his mother entered his room, instantly replacing the TechNahal chat room with the current algebra exercises from the school website. Shira, pretending that she hadn't noticed, crossed the room, sat down, and took his hand.

"I came in to say good night. I want you to know that I do not approve of this spy stuff. But I won't try to stop you." As she held his hand, she idly traced the faint scars on the back of it. "Do you remember? How you got this?"

"Sort of, I guess. I remember being really scared. It was just before Dad died, right?"

"Your father was murdered. He didn't die, he was killed, by terrorists, the same ones who snuck into our apartment— this apartment—and carved an X in your hand, even as I slept in the next room. You were only six. They did it to send a message to us.

"Do you know what I am trying to tell you, Bini? This is no online game. This stuff is real. Israel is always fighting for her life, and none of us can ever be truly safe so long as there are men such as those who did this to you and who killed your father. Your father, as you already know, once worked for Mossad. But he quit and became an emissary of peace, trying to forge links of trade and commerce between Israel and the Palestinians. And still they went after him. They tried to use him, and when he wouldn't cooperate, they killed him."

"Mom, I know all this."

"Yes, you know that much of the story, but the story doesn't end there. Today, I'm wondering where it does end. Who will next kill whom? How many more people have to die?"

"Mom, I'm just playing around with some computers, that's all. Nothing is going to happen. And I'm not a little kid. I'm almost thirteen."

She smiled. "Yes, almost thirteen. But I want you to promise me that you will take this seriously and that you will listen to your Uncle Lev and do exactly what he says. And only what he says."

"Yes, Mom. Now can I get back to my algebra?"

As soon as she was out of the room, Bini toggled back to the chat room.

BwnerPwner:	whasup
HaifaChai5:	momzoid invasion
BwnerPwner:	o gr8
HaifaChai5:	any news bout code txt on ff.org
#Scum:	nancypants sez looks like script 4 sum device, robot or sumthng
HaifaChai5:	shud get hr 2 dconstruct
#Scum:	not OL now, but i cn IM hr
HaifaChai5:	no not IM stick 2 ncryptd chat
BwnerPwner:	i cn tell hr tmrro n skool
HaifaChai5:	kk, all u remember 2 clr logs b4 u lv ff.org & tel me whn nancypants has sumthng

"Got to go," Bini said out loud as he typed G2G and put his computer to sleep.

8

The Internet chatter was spiking again. The Americans had unofficially sent an alert to Lev and his group without giving any specifics, confirming that something seemed to be in the offing. But if they knew any more than the Israelis, they were saying nothing. In principle, at least since 9/11, the CIA and Mossad shared everything; in practice, it was a game of spy-versus-spy, with both agencies playing to win—at the expense of the other if need be. Lev's team, crowded into the small third-floor conference room for an ad hoc strategy session, was trying to tease something new from the wash of Internet noise.

"I'm still thinking Palestinians, Al Aqsa Brigade," said Anat Dorfman, slapping a folder down on the conference table for emphasis. One of two women on the team, she always maintained a tough exterior, something needed in the boys-club atmosphere of her working world. Her face matched her demeanor, with thick eyebrows and strong features, more handsome than pretty. Still, she was attractive enough that more than one of her colleagues had tried unsuccessfully to hit on her. Some speculated that she was butch, but Lev was pretty sure they were wrong, even without any direct evidence to support his hunch.

"It's some major initiative," she said. "We have all that Al Aqsa traffic plus all these separate references to Rajid and—what was the Egyptian?—oh yes, Hamadi. An awful lot must be going on for there to be this kind of a spike. We see only the surface, of course, and assume there is far more buried where we can't track it."

"And who are they? Do we have anything on either of them?" Lev scanned the room as the head shakes swept like a wave around the table. "Then what? What are they up to? Anyone?"

"We are fairly sure from the contexts that this Hamadi is Hamadi el-Masri, known among his contacts simply as The Egyptian. No surprise there," Anat said. "He is well known to us as a facilitator for varied terrorist groups, but we have recently lost track of his whereabouts. He may have been out of the country for a while. At any rate, we don't get this kind of chatter for another wave of suicide strikes. Something's up."

Anat was smart enough, but had a tendency to restate the obvious. Lev never discouraged her, though, because she helped provide the grounding for his team by framing the issues clearly. He nodded in her direction, then looked around the table again.

Pyotr Abramovitch, whose straw-tinged hair and eyes like

blued steel matched his name, raised his index finger. His father had immigrated from Russia with Lev's father. Both had served in the Irgun, and both had moved on to distinguished careers in intelligence. Now their sons carried on in what had become almost a family business of sorts. Pyotr and Anat were the star players in Tech Ops; the others were more like talented functionaries, supporting cast, competent but undistinguished. Lev would have liked to have a few more first-tier players on his team, but given the way Anat and Pyotr could go at each other, there were times that he was grateful to have only the two of them.

"The message may have been devoid of content," Pyotr said, "but we certainly don't get backchannel comm from the Americans over West Bank martyrs, so it must be something else. The Al Aqsa references are puzzling. Perhaps they are shifting tactics to something new, something bigger."

Just then, Rahel opened the door to the conference room, banging into the back of Pyotr's chair.

"*Slicha*. Sorry to interrupt, but Rafi Yadin's on the phone for you, Lev," she said. Lev told his team to continue without him and excused himself.

A call from Yadin was an occasion. Yadin was Lev's closest counterpart at Shin Bet, Israel's domestic intelligence service—its unseen shield, as they styled themselves. Although no one would acknowledge overt competition or openly claim any lack of cooperation, there would always be a certain amount of territorial posturing and positioning among the three branches of Israeli intelligence. As a practical matter, Lev's work did not often give him much reason to deal with anyone at Aman, the military intelligence group, but he knew Yadin and his team at Shin Bet fairly well.

"To what do I attribute the honor of your call?" he said, picking up the phone in his office.

"Can you meet me at the *Sha'arei Tzedek* Medical Center in an hour? I have something to show you."

"Can you tell me anything more?"

"Not yet. But this might have some connection with some channels we have both been monitoring."

"I see. I'll show you mine if you show me yours. Right?"

"Just come to the hospital, and we'll talk once you see what we are dealing with."

<hr>

At the Medical Center, Lev parked in the covered portion of the parking facility, walked up two flights to the broad plaza, and jogged toward the gleaming white arms of the main building. *Sha'arei Tzedek* in central Jerusalem was more than just a simple hospital. It was a complete campus. As an affiliate of Hebrew University, it had become a major center of teaching and research, and as a hospital it had earned a reputation for first-rate treatment without consideration for ethnic or religious distinctions. Palestinians and Ultraorthodox Israelis, Christian visitors and secular residents, were all accommodated equally. The hospital with a heart was how it was known to its supporters and to many of its patients and ex-patients.

Rafi had left a message at the front desk, and Lev tracked him down in a remote wing of an underground part of the complex. He was standing outside an isolation room, watching as a nurse in full surgical garb and mask attended to a skinny, dark-skinned boy nestled in a tangle of intravenous tubes and cables.

"That's Habib," Rafi said, nodding. "He was transferred here from Beit Jala in an armored ambulance this morning after they diagnosed acute radiation sickness. Those lesions on his arm, I am told those are actual radiation burns from skin contact. Cesium-137, they think, not sure yet. And you? You are wondering why we are standing here watching a nine-year-old Palestinian kid fighting for his life." He paused for dramatic effect.

"He is the second one this week; his house is fifty meters from the house of the other boy. We are trying to find out what we can, but the neighborhood comes under the Palestinian Authority. We are pushing for a house-to-house search, but we do not want to tip our hand to the other side, and the Authority can sometimes be less than diligent in investigating their own, so ..."

"And what do you think this has to do with us?" Lev asked.

"You tell us. We picked up a plaintext posting on a social networking site that referenced the neighborhood where he and the other boy lived. We know you have been watching the site. Fill me in."

"Rafi, I would if I could. You know that, but we have nothing, just chatter, some names, and a useless heads-up from the Americans."

"Okay, then, the names."

"Only one, really," he lied. "Hamadi el-Masri, one of the usual suspects. At least we assume that's the Hamadi that keeps coming up in channels we are monitoring. But we don't know what he might be up to, and we don't know where he is at the moment. I assume you, too, have been picking up the flood of references to Al Aqsa."

Rafi nodded. "Is it just you and your high-tech analysts or is anyone out in the field working this one?"

"We have our *katsas*. We have everyone we can on this one, but it's just noise in the circuit so far, and we have other priorities, as well you know. We also have that university student from England who was shot. She's here, you know, at the Center, upstairs. Last I heard it wasn't clear whether she would make it or not. We still don't know who was behind the attack."

"We know who."

"What? You know? Who?"

"The IDF. It was one of their bullets."

"Not funny, Rafi. Really, tell me what you have. What's in the offing?"

"Off the record? No substance, but our people are starting to think RDD, radiological dispersion device, especially now that these boys show up with radiation poisoning."

"Dirty bomb? Is that what you're thinking? Can't we just send in a hazmat team to sweep the whole area?"

"Not without cooperation from the Palestinians and not without tipping our hand on the whole radioactivity angle. We don't want to scare them into going to ground."

"What if we lied, let it leak that the boys had some kind of chemical poisoning or maybe some biohazard, hemorrhagic fever of some kind—an excuse to offer our help and send in a squad in white suits and breathers? It could work. What do you think?"

"Worth a try, I suppose, although the word is probably already out from Beit Jala."

"Then I would say get it done yesterday," Lev said, with evident impatience, "before the word is more out. It's your territory, not mine. And we'll step up our operations, such as they are. You did not hear this from me, but we do know a deal went down recently in Eastern Europe. No details, but substantial cash has been suddenly showing up in border villages where there shouldn't be any. We are working on it and may have some names soon."

"Okay," Rafi nodded to acknowledge the bonus information. "So, we have another clue for you, then, although we have not a clue as to what it means. Pox. It's been flagged as an infrequent and unlikely word that keeps coming up in tracked West Bank email. Mean anything to you?"

"No. But I'll ask my boys and girls to work on it, too. Let's go."

As the two men headed back toward the elevator, a young woman hesitantly entered the hallway from a stairwell and quietly approached the observation window from the other direction. For nearly an hour, Najat stood and watched her cousin Habib. She had only seen him twice before, but he was family, and his welfare was a matter of family concern. She watched his breathing, its precise, mechanized rhythm almost hypnotic, like the chanting of her uncle at prayer and the relentless logic of his radical friends: pumping, pushing, breathing life and determination. She would have stayed longer, watching, wondering over the near and far future, but she had business, and there would be stops and many checkpoints and buses before she would be finished and back to the campus.

At his office in Tel Aviv, Lev summoned Rahel. "With *Shabak* potentially splashing in our pond," he said, using the complete acronym for Shin Bet, "we need to make the case for full disclosure in both directions. Courier the file on Operation Chit-Chat to Yadin."

"Really? The whole file?" she said, nervously pulling on a

few stray strands of hair, as she tended to do whenever talking with Lev. Lev, trained as he was, knew the significance of the unconscious gesture. He deliberately brushed back a lock of his own rebellious hair. Keep the connection live, he thought.

"No, of course not," he said. "Just give them enough real information so they feel that we are sincere and that they are getting something out of us." She started to leave. "Wait, while you are at it, let's give military intelligence a heads up just in case. Confirm who is now my counterpart in Aman and fire off an FYI. Ask if they are getting any new intelligence about nuclear options." Rahel's eyebrows shot up. "And don't do that. It's inappropriate in a spy," he teased. She stuck out her tongue for a tiny fraction of a second, but enough to get Lev thinking.

He was still thinking when Anat drummed her fingers on his door jamb, stepped into the office without waiting for an acknowledgement, and placed a folder on his desk. "It's a long shot, but I was doing a rundown on the name Rajid. It's a pretty long list, although not as long as for Hamadi. Still this is just a preliminary once-over for anyone who might stand out in some way. Of course, we have the famous footballer, but that's a non-starter. Then there's a Gaza civil rights leader. We are already working on that and a few other angles. But this is the one I wanted to flag for your attention, a Rajid Bannerjee who applied for a tourist visa to Israel, for a conference next week." She flipped open the folder. "Seems he is headed for a computer conference at the Technion. Want me to go do some digging?"

"Yes." He shook his head. "No. Do whatever you can from your desk, but I have another angle for the conference itself. Besides, it's domestic and we don't want to step into Shin Bet territory, at least not too openly." He gestured for her to sit down, then dialed a number from memory.

"Karl, it's Lev," he said into the phone. "How would you like to actually earn your keep and do a little favor for me. There is a conference coming up at the Technion." He read from the note Anat handed him, "The Third International A2C4, Advanced Applications of Collaborative, Convergent, and Cloud Computing. Sounds really, really fascinating, eh? I think you should cover it for your blog or whatever rag you are writing for these days and check out someone named Rajid Bannerjee for me. Okay? Details later."

He put down the phone and looked over to Anat, who had a puzzled look on her face.

"That was Karl Lustig. He married the widow of my best friend, one of the best agents we have ever had, by the way, although also something of a renegade. Karl is an amateur, of course, but good—methodical and tenacious. Once he gets his teeth into a lead he'll hang on like a hungry jackal. Still, track all his comm for me and keep me posted."

Lev spent the afternoon staring at his screen and shuffling paper. He was about to call it quits when internal email arrived from Shimon Weiszkopf. It was an edited and processed transcript from the logger planted in Bini's computer. Most of the noise and garbage had already been filtered out, leaving Bini's sessions with TechNahal, his Web surfing, and his visits to FaceFolder.org highlighted. Lev scanned the first few TechNahal sessions, then cursed when he got to one with a sudden change in content. "The little bugger," he said out loud. "What is he up to?"

I wonder if he's online now? Lev thought. He ran through

the possibilities. Skype perhaps? Worth a try. Sure enough, there he is. Same handle as for the TechNahal chat room. He's devious but hasn't learned all the tricks. Not yet, anyway. I think I'll try voice rather than chat, keep it nice, informal. Ring-a-ding, Bini, ring-a-ding.

Bini answered on the fourth ring. "Hello? Who is this? Your ID is blocked somehow. I didn't know they could do that on Skype." There was a hesitance in the voice on the other end of the connection, as if Bini wasn't sure whether he should be taking a Skype call from a stranger, particularly a stranger with a blocked ID.

Lev hesitated for a moment, then decided to plunge ahead. "It's your Uncle Lev. I want to know what you're up to and why. You and your friends suddenly started talking in code. What gives?" There was a pause and the sound of a door closing and then the scraping of a chair.

"I, well, how did you ...? Oh, wow, like I get it. Of course. We just didn't know it was you. I mean, once I found this Trojan on my system, I thought maybe the other side had penetrated our defenses, which I didn't think was, like, possible, you know. Yeah. We left it in place because we were worried about tipping them off."

Lev shook his head in disbelief. "You found out about our spyware?" he said.

"Well, yes. Sure. I can tell if anything is ever added to my system. I run extra external checksums on all my software and have three layers of freeware anti-virus protection. So when it looked like something had slipped in, I rigged up a packet sniffer to track all my traffic on the network, and it became obvious. Somebody was snooping and sending it all home. Except I couldn't find out who owned the IP address that messages were going out to, and it kept changing, so I figured it must be the bad guys. But it was you, right? I should have known. Anyway, we all decided to play it cool and chat in code after that."

"All right. So you can stop talking in code. I note your chat room is itself encrypted, so the bad guys aren't going to be listening in, not on a bunch of kids, anyway, unless you do something stupid to get their attention on FaceFolder.org, and I'll trust that none of you is stupid.

"So, fill me in, Bini. What's up?"

"Well, okay, so maybe you already know that Nancypants, that's her handle—I'm not sure I know her real name—well, she's a vo-tech student. You know what that means? Well, she goes to a vocational-technical school outside of Boston, and they have, like, everything. Well, she says that this script we found on one of their servers is something like CNC code—computer numerical control—for machine tools or industrial robots or something, but different. She is still trying to make sense of it. She's good, older, maybe sixteen, I think. She has even programmed a five-axis milling machine, which is, well I'm not sure exactly, but it's hairy. Anyway, there are no comments and no source text for this script, at least that we can find, so it's mostly just codes and numbers. But she and Boner, er, well, that's what we call him because, well, not for that reason, but because NancyPants says he acts like a real bonehead in class even though he's brilliant. So, she and Boner have been writing a de-compiler to translate this script, making guesses and stuff and doing pattern matching. And ..."

"Wait, Bini. Just tell me if you've found anything, anything that might be useful, anything at all, even if it doesn't mean much to you."

"Well, yes, that's what I was going to tell you. But, are you sure this is alright to talk like this?"

"Trust me. For one, Skype traffic is all encrypted, anyway; for two, it's peer-to-peer, scattered all over the place, isolated packets bouncing around among all the users online; and for three, it all vanishes the moment a packet gets passed on. There's a fourth one, but I can't tell you about that for security reasons. So, believe me, we can talk. So talk."

"Right. See we have figured out some of the code. Some loops. One looks like an inner loop that keeps testing against two values and eventually triggers a series of input-output modules, actuators or something, like turning some things off. Or on. We just found the same two eight-digit numbers in two other places in the code. Just numbers, but like a little weird, I mean, like, eight-digit precision? So we figured they must be important. I can email them to you, if you want, Uncle Lev."

"No, no email. Not until we can get you set up with encryption, I mean real encryption, which maybe we should do. Do you have the numbers at hand? Can you just read them to me?"

"Sure," Bini said, clicking to another window and scrolling down through several pages. "Here they are. Got a pencil? One is 35.235422, the other is 31.778003. Mean anything?"

"No, but we also have our own smart kids here. I'll get some of them working on it. Oh, and Bini, don't tell your friends about our logger. Just tell them you were able to quarantine the virus, so there's no need to speak in code anymore. Okay?"

"Sure, Uncle Lev. This is pretty cool, huh? I'm working with you. Just like my father."

"Right." Right, just like your father. Migdal, oh Migdal,

do forgive me. "Right. Just be careful. And say nothing about this, not to anybody. Bye."

Lev stared at the numbers. Two numbers. A pair of numbers. What numbers come in pairs, he wondered. Coordinates. Latitude and longitude? He opened a browser, brought up Google Maps, and entered the numbers as coordinates. The map was a featureless blue, somewhere at sea. He switched to satellite view and zoomed back until he could see that the spot was not far off the West coast of Cypress. A rendezvous in the Mediterranean? Who knows. Wait a minute. Maybe I had them backwards. 32 north and 35 east should be someplace in Israel. So, let's turn them around. He retyped the numbers and hit return. The image leaped. He zoomed in and in.

Fuck. We got problems. Big problems. Al Aqsa. Now I see, it was not the name of the group, not the Martyrs Brigade. He bit his lip as he reached for his secure phone. He was staring down at the exact center of *Kipat HaSela*, the Dome of the Rock on the Temple Mount.

9

Rajid pulled back the tarp and inspected the handi-work, caressing the flat finish, and admiring the cus-tom camouflage paint. He had carefully managed and monitored the project throughout, but now would have only this one last chance to verify the construction. More than one visit would risk attracting too much attention. It had been moved twice already, disassembled, dispersed among couriers, then finally reassembled. Only he and a handful of highly trusted accomplices had even seen the thing whole. He had paid well for silence and assistance and had fanned the flames of a deeper loyalty, flames fueled by religious fervor and by hatred. Still, there was always the risk of a slip, or of usurpers or competitors hoping to use his work to their own ends. Along the long road to this remote spot in the hills some had died, some had disappeared, and large sums of money had changed hands. All of these had been necessary milestones along the way. Even the deaths had served their purposes, helping to cement loyalties and securing dedication among those still left behind.

Rajid connected a cable to his laptop and plugged the other end into a socket under a discreetly located sliding cover. He typed a command, and his hand-crafted software started running through a complex and lengthy set of diagnostics. The others stood and stared, silently praying. Other than the wind, the only sounds were of clicking relays, spinning disk drives, and an occasional thump of an actuator or a double grunt of a servomotor pulsed briefly, ever so briefly, first one way, then the other. Signal lights beside the connector socket flickered, and line after line of text scrolled up and off the laptop screen faster than any of the watchers could follow. At last the laptop chimed and the screen displayed a message: Diagnostics Complete. All Tests Passed. Rajid stood, stretched, and tugged the tarp back into place.

The hot wind rustled the tops of the olive trees and swirled dust around the feet of the two men standing by the narrow track. Ahmad gravely shook hands with Rajid.

"As was agreed, then," Ahmad said. "We are united in a cause, joined by our hatred of the Zionist devils. Is it not so?" He paused.

Or perhaps, thought Rajid, we are joined by the substantial sum of money now in the pocket of your robe. He nodded to reassure Ahmad, smiled, and gestured for him to continue.

"We have built it as you asked," Ahmad said. "Your engineering drawings were good, of course, most good. But we could not actually test it, as you must know. There is no place, no facility in which to do that. As it was, we were fabricating it here, and in Ramallah, and in a little shop near Nablus. Now it has been assembled and is ready for your use. For our use. But, we could not test it."

Rajid nodded. "We know. There will be no need. We trust you and your dedication to make it perfect, that it may become the Sword of the Prophet." And, of course, we trust our own engineering, he thought. That and our particular project management philosophy.

The whole effort had been conservatively designed with rather wide tolerances, and many of the parts were "Commercial Off-The-Shelf" systems. Using COTS wherever possible cut risks and saved everyone time and money. Nothing too exotic, of course, all so-called dual-use components. In the end, there had been no choice but to trust the resourcefulness of Ahmad and his collaborators to use their own networks and discretion to acquire the components quietly, over time. And, of course, not everything rested on Ahmad; he was not alone.

"As to the supply chain, Ahmad, we know you were on your own, but it seems you did not need our help in any case, which we could not have given, in any case, for reasons I am certain were most clear to you. Even now—especially now—there must be no attention drawn to our project, as you understand so well."

Ahmad nodded and said, "It is so. Salaam."

"Salaam," Rajid replied. "I will be in touch again when we are ready, when it is time. You know what is required." He crossed the road and restarted his dirt-smeared Volkswagen. It would be a long and dusty ride to his next meeting, where he would see another team working from another set of plans and run another set of diagnostics. It will work, he thought. No test, no rehearsal. Neither is possible, neither is necessary. We know what we are doing.

A pile of rubble—potshards, broken bits of brick, and shattered stones—blocked the way ahead. The scene, made at once both garish and ghostly by the low-light enhancement of the special camera, did not look encouraging. A double-jointed mechanical arm reached out and started to lift chunks of debris and move them aside, slowly revealing a dark triangle low in the wall. As the work progressed, the dark shape could be seen to be an opening into a further passage. Even after it was finally exposed completely, the opening appeared much too small to pass through.

The arm pulled back. A series of quick clicks and short whines was followed by the arm extending again, this time with one long finger outstretched, pointing, a finger that began to turn as it approached the wall above the opening. A spray of dust and chips flew out in every direction as the spinning finger drilled into the masonry wall. It withdrew to reveal a neat hole half a meter above the low opening. Again the arm retracted, and again the clicks and whines. This time the arm returned into view holding a rod that it lined up and pushed expertly into the hole in the wall. More whining, and the scene contracted as the camera pulled back, farther and farther. Then nothing. The image could have been a still photograph. Only the sound of random clicks and quiet scrapings proved that the link was still live. Then it began. A rhythmic subtle shaking of the image and a sound in the distance, a quiet rumbling and rattling like heavy traffic passing overhead. As if this were an awaited signal, the world spun suddenly as the camera panned rapidly away from the dark hole and the protruding rod above it. There was a sharp whack, like someone slapping a bed, and the camera swung back to face a roiling cloud of dust. The dust suddenly disappeared, to be replaced by a grainy false-color image of the wall as the near-infra-red camera was turned on to cut through the dust. A fresh pile of rubble now lay ahead, but the hole had been enlarged considerably. The image slowly grew larger again, and the arm began the tedious task of clearing the debris from the blast. With the path finally cleared, the camera lumbered toward and through the opening. The image once again returned to visible light, revealing a very large room with a vaulted ceiling of crisscrossing arches.

"Wow," said Bini softly, as he shifted back from full screen view to expose another window on the desktop. He clicked on the save button to store the captured video stream, then posted it to the TechNahal file area. Despite compression, the file was enormous and would take many minutes to upload. As the progress bar inched across the window, Bini composed a message to his TechNahal friends.

"Tapping into the live feed from the camera was brilliant, Boner," he wrote, deliberately practicing writing out his posts in full text, "but we'll never be able to capture and save all the streaming video. We should, you know, take advantage of being in different time zones and establish a schedule to monitor the feed and save only bits that look interesting. Like this one. Something bothers me, though. I ask you, should archeologists be blowing holes in walls? I mean, it's a dig, right?"

He switched to another window where he flipped through the maps and plots he had downloaded from the archeology site. He went through them all several times. The tunnel in the

last video images was not on the maps. This had happened before. The maps were automatically updated as the little robots
explored and sent back data, and the 3D virtual renderings
that allowed one to visually navigate the network of inter-
connected tunnels and caverns were generated within a day or
two afterwards. But the video stream that Boner had managed
to tap into never seemed to make it into the renderings or onto
the maps.

Curiouser and curiouser, thought Bini. He added a note at
the end of his message: "Check the maps and tell me what you
think."

"Why are we here?" Gillian asked. She looked around the tunnel. "This is for tourists." She was with Harold in the Western
Wall Tunnels that had been excavated after the Six Day War
in order to expose and give public access to the full length of
the remains of the Western Wall of the Temple. Concealed
lighting cast the walls into dramatic relief and discreet signs
marked points of interest. Ahead, the small tour group of
Americans, along with a few Germans and a couple of Rus-
sians, was just rounding the corner. Harold, his hand on Gillian's back, gently urged her forward.

"Think of it as a busman's holiday. Or an archeologist's
holiday. What else would we do on our day off except go underground? Only this time, we get to go ourselves, in the
flesh." He gave her a brief squeeze around the waist. "A lot
better than just watching a screen and fiddling with a joy
stick." He reached for her hand, grabbed her thumb, and made
twisting, rocking motions as if controlling one of the robots.
She laughed and looked up at him, inclining her head playfully, as if to lean on his shoulder but stopping just a few centi-

meters short.

Harold loved this game, the playful pretenses, the escalating near misses, the frightening tension between moving too fast and missing an opening. He gave a quick squeeze to her hand before letting go and stepping over to an engraved plaque. It was written in English as well as Hebrew, but Harold, never missing a chance to show off, read the Hebrew aloud, then did his own translation.

"We are at a point opposite what is believed to have been the site of the Holy of Holies, the closest spot to what was once the heart of the temple before it was destroyed. Or so they say. Would you believe, Jews are officially prohibited from being within the reconstructed boundaries of the original temple? Rabbinical authorities argue that all modern Jews must be considered by definition to be ritually impure and therefore not allowed entry to the Temple. We, of course, are under no such prohibition, being under the New Covenant of our Lord and Savior." He bowed his head and clasped his hands as if making a quick prayer.

"And I wonder what the rabbinical authorities would make of our little robot friends," he said, turning back to Gillian. "Do you think maybe we should put little beanies on them?" She tried, unsuccessfully, not to giggle. Harold put his hands on her shoulders as he joined in her sniggering.

Enough, he thought. Don't overdo it for today. He withdrew his hands slowly and looked at them briefly in a move that might have passed for reluctance or even embarrassment but was actually his savoring the fading sense of the warmth from her in his palms.

"Shadrach has been closer to the putative location of the Ark than this," she said, breaking the awkward silence. "At last by my calculations, anyway."

"You're right. And be thankful that the summary report of our exploratory mapping will not reach certain concerned groups until long after we are finished here. Of course, there are other routes, and we are not the only ones to explore this area underground. Rumors persist that there is a gate in these very tunnels, someplace beyond the public areas, that leads directly under the Dome of the Rock.

"But, enough shop talk. Let's catch up with our tour guide. We can see if we can catch him making any false claims or historical blunders. He may be cute, but he is not all that smart."

"Not all that cute, either," she said. "I don't think these Hebrews are really my type." She looked demurely down as she finished, as if making a revealing confession.

Harold's heart began to pound in his chest. "Okay. After this, let's go for a walk, just explore for a bit, above ground for a change. Then tonight, I will treat you to dinner at this really great little Lebanese restaurant I discovered. I don't know about you, but I have had quite enough kosher food for now. So ..."

"Come on, let's catch up," she said, taking his hand and pulling him along.

Yes, Harold thought, yes indeed.

10

Like a salmon swimming against the current, Karl made his way across the Technion campus, heading upstream back toward the Taub Computer Science Building as the crowd facing him edged toward the Churchill Auditorium for the opening plenary of the conference. It was a deliberate tactic, a trick he had developed as a journalist that allowed him to gauge the crowd, scan for people he knew, and easily read the badges of those he didn't. This crowd was a sea of strangers, and the name tags were as unfamiliar as the faces. He realized he was going to be a bit out of his depth on this assignment and would have to work to find an angle for any posting he might write.

Thank you, Lev Novikov, he thought. Just what I needed.

Suddenly, he recognized the name on a badge and started trying to figure out how he knew it. He raised his eyes to look into the impatient face of an elderly gentleman with mutton-chop sideburns and piercing eyes, a distinctive and unforgettable face that Karl immediately recalled having seen on a book jacket, in fact, on quite a few book jackets.

"Hargrove? Clarkson Hargrove, the writer. Am I right?"

The man scowled slightly and said, "Do we know each other?"

"No, not really, although I get the feeling that we may have met once before. But I do know your work, of course. I'm Karl Lustig. I write for iTech Weekly, online edition," he said, reflexively fingering the badge clipped to his jacket. "I'm covering the conference. But I must say, I hardly would have expected you at a conference like this."

"Do please tell me why not," the man said. Annoyance spread from his bushy eyebrows down, like a window shade being drawn over his face.

"Well, I just don't connect massively parallel distributed computation with your writing. I mean, my twelve-year-old son reads your books."

"Oh, really? Your son studies medieval history and the emergence of modernism in Western scientific thought?"

"No, of course not. Please forgive my gaff. It's so easy to forget you're a scholar as well as a popular author. Naturally, I meant *The Princes of Pelucida*. My son, Binyamin, has read every one of the series. Your books have done wonders for his mastery of English.

"His favorite character is Shimji, the Crafter. I know because he told me he was very angry when you killed him off in the last book. He owns all nine in the—what would you call it?—the triple trilogy."

"Well, good for your son. And for my bank balance. I am grateful, and my accountant shall be grateful as well, I am sure. But I fear you are in error. Your son has not read them all, not yet."

"But the last one, *Battle at Harjhan*, it was a virtual Armageddon, the end of the world and plainly billed as the last book in the series. Rather a bit gruesome, too, I would say, not at all what I would usually consider fare for children."

"Young adults, sir. The category is called 'young adult fiction' as you can verify by walking into any decent bookseller and looking at the signs posted above the shelves. I write young adult fiction. I cannot be held responsible for the wayward children who inappropriately get their hands on my books and then find themselves in over their heads any more than I can be held to account for the incompetent or neglectful parents who permit them such ill-conceived choices."

Karl was taken aback, but persisted. "I suppose, but, see, my son and I often read aloud to each other, and it would seem that when Shimji gets his revenge on the Theochrons by poisoning the Well of Delusion with his own rotting remains, the deaths of their young children were described in somewhat excessive detail, wouldn't you say?"

"I would not. But, then, I am the author, am I not. Perhaps I shall be redeemed by the final volume."

"But wait, I seem to recall you saying in a BBC interview that you would never write another. I also recall protests by youngsters around the world. Seems they always want more."

"So it would seem. And they shall have it. The series was always planned as a Decalogue. I thought everyone knew. Ten words or ten things, *aseret ha-devarim,* as you say in Hebrew.

Not ten commandments, as the Christians always garble it. For you of the Hebrew persuasion, of course, it is rather more complicated than two hands worth: 613 commandments in all, if I recall correctly. Nevertheless, I had always thought my epigraphs were rather transparent, even with the occasional inversions—or perversions, as my critics like to say—of the original text. 'You shall have no gods before you.' Rather plain, I would say, and so much more sensible than the original. The International Skeptics League, of which I am a lifetime member, and RAAAA, the Radical Association for Atheist and Agnostic Action—one must admire their acronymic exuberance—have both been rather enthusiastic about the conceit and, indeed, about the whole series." He paused, reflecting for a moment.

"In any event, your son can already place an advance order for the next book on Amazon.co.uk, so, you see, it must be real." He flashed a quick blink of a smile. "Of course, my publishers are doing all they can at the moment to make a royal mess of matters. They keep telling me I cannot end the series as I have chosen and are insisting I rewrite the final three chapters. But what do they know of Pelucida or of creative fiction, eh? I am both smarter and more stubborn than they are. In the end, I will prevail, and the world will end exactly as I planned, as and when it should.

"And speaking of endings, I must end this interruption. Do forgive my haste, but I really do not want to miss the opening ceremonies." He started to edge back into the surging crowd, and Karl turned to follow.

"Of course, of course. But I am still curious about your interest in this particular conference. What is the connection with massive parallel computation?"

"Look," he said, sighing deeply. "I really do have nothing whatsoever against journalists, apart from despising their very existence, that is, and wishing every Janus-faced one of them were banished to some distant and barren planet. As to your curiosity, aside from my somewhat embarrassing but most rewarding pastime of penning a few pieces for juveniles, I do have what you Americans—and I do beg forgiveness if that is an unwarranted extrapolation from your accent—what you Americans refer to as a day job, to wit, the history of humanism in the modern rational worldview."

"You definitely have an ear for language," Karl said. "Yes, I'm American, although I've lived in Haifa for years now."

"As I was saying," Hargrove continued, "with two of my students, I just completed a massive content analysis of the entire online corpus of digitized medieval and renaissance literature and commentary thereon. We recruited—or commandeered, if you prefer—some 4,100 personal computers, a virtual bot brigade, in the ugly vernacular, for background computation of a comprehensive multilingual concordance. You may have heard of the project? SETI. The Search for Evidence of Terrestrial Intelligence." He exhaled sharply. "I jest, of course. That search is still ongoing, is it not?"

"Ah, a di-jest," Karl punned.

Hargrove ignored him and continued. "Regardless, our completed project is being reported here by my students. In the doctoral consortium on Thursday, should you be interested."

"I thank you, kind sir," Karl said with a nod, "for your patience in explaining your presence and clarifying your perspective on my profession." Karl bowed just a centimeter or two. "With your kind permission, then, I will take my leave now and go in search of a suitably distant and barren planet for my banishment. I do hope you enjoy the conference. Cheers."

Hargrove did not reply but merely turned into the crowd without further comment or acknowledgment. Karl stood there realizing his polite sarcasm had been completely wasted. With no interest in the largely ceremonial first session, he looked around for a place to sit and check his email. There was a bench just off the path, so he sat down, booted up, and was rewarded by a solid, four-bar Wi-Fi signal. Most of the email he downloaded had nearly identical subject lines, all of them rants from angry readers in response to a recent posting of his on what he had called "ham-fisted human factors" in certain modern software engineering tools.

People could be so sectarian about software. It always amazed Karl how professionals could become so invested in a favorite tool or preferred operating system. Religious fanatics had nothing on computer geeks arguing about the Mac OS versus Microsoft Windows or Ruby on Rails versus Java. Amidst the diatribes and invective in his inbox, there was a single PGP encrypted message. Karl entered his private key and read the single word message from Lev: call.

He looked around. Everyone else was already in the auditorium, so he flipped open his cellphone and dialed Lev's direct line. Lev picked up on the first ring. "Anything on this Rajid character?" he asked without waiting for a word from Karl.

"Nothing," Karl said, "Not yet. I just got here. He's not on the program and there are several hundred delegates. Give me a little time."

"We may not have that luxury. Your son and his pals have stumbled onto something. I want you to Google Map this pair of numbers and tell me what you see in the satellite view." He read them out slowly.

There was a pause of many seconds, then one word: "Shit."

"You see shit, do you?"

"No, I see disaster, with a capital D, for Dome. Is this the target."

"We don't know yet," said Lev. "But it's a good guess. We've been here before, you know. We once foiled a plot by the Kahane Kach Party to blow up the Dome of the Rock, so this would not be the first time. As to who has picked it out this time, we do not even have guesses, which is why we need something on your man. Otherwise we will have to resort to cruder methods. Work smart, Karl, and work fast. Okay?"

Karl took a breath. "If you don't want me to do this, then fine. But if you do, then give me a chance. I'll find him. If not today, then tonight at the conference reception. I am pretty good at puzzles, remember? Let me puzzle this one out."

"Right. We are just getting anxious here. I can't say more, but if you can get something out of this guy, get it. Now." The phone clicked.

So much for telephone courtesy, thought Karl. He switched back to his inbox filled with angry emails and thought again of his encounter with Clarkson Hargrove. It was certainly not proving to be the day for polite dialogue.

11

At conferences, Hargrove always sat on the aisle, toward the back of the room, just in case the session bored or annoyed him, which it often did, sometimes enough for him to raise his hand and enliven the proceedings with the intellectual thrust and parry of an academic joust, but more often only enough to give him cause to leave early. The afternoon's presentation, on an obscure new theory of depth versus breadth in distributed search algorithms, had held his interest through the second PowerPoint slide, in which the two graduate students presented their formula, a formula that Hargrove saw as patently unoriginal and not nearly as general as his own unpublished work on the subject. The fact that his work was still not in print deprived Hargrove of the chance to score points on the presenters by drawing attention to their failure to do a thorough search of the literature. Cursing the reviewers at *Subtext: The Journal of Narrative Analytics* for having delayed his manuscript through two rounds of revision—both wholly unnecessary in his mind—Hargrove rose from his seat and slipped out of one of the side doors. He let it close behind him just loudly enough to make his egress evident as a nonverbal commentary for the now nearly drowning student presenters who, by their third slide, had lost the rest of the audience. Of course, it also was a wordless rebuke for the bulk of the attendees who were more willing than Hargrove to soldier on in polite boredom. Civil cowardice, he called it. Better, he thought, if the audience walked out *en masse* as a valuable and unforgettable lesson to the inept and immature pair of presenters. Now, while they are young, is the best time for them to learn these vital life lessons. Otherwise, they shall end up like my universally despised colleague, the ever vacuous and perpetually boring Professor Warwick.

As the bang of the heavy door echoed, two men in jeans and leather jackets, one tall and swarthy, the other short and ruddy, rose from a bench farther down the hall and hurried to intercept his path. Hargrove, unsure as to whether to be on his guard under the circumstances, stiffened as the two approached.

"Are you Clarkson Hargrove?"

Hargrove made a show of fingering his conference badge and said, "So it says here on my badge, I do believe, in an easily read typeface. Last time I checked, it still stated that I was Clarkson Daniel Hargrove. Is there something I can do for you, uh, gentlemen?"

"Do you know a Clarissa Hargrove?"

"I do, as a matter of fact. My niece. Although I can't say that I know her very well, since my brother and I are not, shall we say, very close. Why do you ask? Is the girl in some kind of trouble?" The last time he had seen her, she had been a gangly teenager, quiet and shy to the point of painful awkwardness. His brother had a way of sapping all confidence and grace from those around him, not least of all his own child. Hargrove disapproved of the way his brother raised the girl, as he disapproved of the way his brother did almost everything, beginning with the marriage to a Danish violinist who was all talent and no brains and ending with the recent divorce. He should have listened to me, Hargrove thought. That would have been a first.

"No, your niece is not in trouble," the taller of the two men said, "but there has been an accident, an incident. She is in hospital. We have contacted the British Embassy, and we have been informed that they have reached her family, but, since we learned you were already here, we thought you might want to see her."

"Yes, yes of course," Hargrove said, adopting a note of sincerity appropriate to the circumstances. "Where is she?"

"In Jerusalem, we'll take you there."

"And who exactly is 'we' in this instance?" he asked, eyeing their casual attire.

"I am sorry. We're with the police. Detective Shimshon and this is Detective Roth," he said, gesturing toward his shorter companion. They showed Hargrove their badge holders in perfect synchrony.

"Well, then, I suppose we had better be off," he said.

The ride to Jerusalem might as well have been by taxi. Neither of the men spoke again once they had ushered him into the back of an unmarked car. He had a moment of anxiety about the authenticity of his escorts until he noticed the lack of inside door handles in the back, which both reassured him and raised his discomfort at the same time.

As they approached the hospital, the car followed the route marked for authorized vehicles only and swung around toward the rear of the sprawling hospital. The two policeman jumped out of the vehicle smartly, as if part of a practiced drill team, opened the door for Hargrove, gestured, then waited impatiently for him to exit. As much to assert autonomy as to express resentment over the silent transport, Hargrove took his time getting out. He stood, brushed at the wrinkles in his crumpled suit jacket, and straightened his tie before nodding to the policeman.

"This way," Detective Shimshon said, taking the lead with Roth trailing behind Hargrove.

They led him through a maze of hospital hallways to an elevator, then to a secured floor. After being ushered past guards, Hargrove found himself in an intensive care room, looking down at an unrecognizable young woman. He was suddenly acutely aware of how distant he had been from his brother's family. His niece, haloed by tubes and monitoring cables, was a young woman with chestnut hair and a somewhat horsey English face, not pretty but not unattractive either. She could have been one of the earnest students in his graduate seminars. Aside from an obscenely large bandage above and half-obscuring her left eye, she looked fine, as if peacefully sleeping.

"Harel, I'm Doctor Harel!" said a voice behind him.

Hargrove turned to see a pudgy man in a white smock enter the room, arm stiffly extended for a handshake as he approached.

"I'm Doctor Harel, and you must be the uncle. I am glad you are here. I understand your brother arrives from London early tomorrow morning. I am so sorry. We have done everything, of course. Still, if I can speak frankly. May I speak frankly?"

Taken aback, Hargrove hesitated. "Ah, yes, I suppose. Of course."

"We cannot be optimistic. Naturally, in medicine, nothing is certain. But. There was extensive brain damage. The bullet entered above her left eye, exited through her neck, and lodged in her shoulder. The hydrostatic pressure of the impact—the bullet had traveled a very long arc—should have, or I should say *could* have, nearly exploded her head, but it did not. She is alive only because of the quick work of an emergency medical technician from the *Magen David Adom* and an American doctor who just happened to be nearby. A miracle, I suppose, of a sort."

"It does not sound very miraculous, even if one is inclined to believe in miracles, which I most decidedly am not. You are saying she is brain dead?"

"A layman's term, brain dead. No, but given the extent of the damage, the odds of a recovery from such a vegetative state are, shall we say, extremely remote. And, in that unlikely event, she would be seriously," he paused as if pondering the perfect choice of words, "impaired. For now, she is on a respirator that is keeping her alive."

"If one can call that alive." Hargrove exhaled sharply. "Tell me, what happened, precisely?"

Detective Roth, standing in discreet silence in the doorway, cleared his throat and approached. "There was an attack by terrorists, two gunmen from a Palestinian splinter group. It was actually quite far from where your niece was. Members of the IDF, the Israeli Defense Forces, had received a fore-warning, and sharpshooters were in place atop a nearby build-ing. As military investigators have told us—and nothing is official or final as yet, understand—one of our soldiers was shot and discharged his firearm into the air as he fell from the building. Ballistics suggest that the bullet that struck your niece was from his weapon. Thankfully, the soldier survived the fall and there were no other casualties. Except the ter-rorists. They were killed. Needless to say."

"Needless to say."

"Well, yes. Our men are good shots."

"Especially when they are shooting at British tourists."

"I said, it was an accidental discharge."

"Yes, accidental, but in a context in which the distinction between accident and intention almost ceases to have meaning or relevance." He turned to look at his niece, the young wom-an he barely knew and now would never know. For the briefest of moments, a shiver ran through him before he composed himself again. "I would appreciate it if you would drive me back to my hotel, officer."

"Detective. It's Detective Roth. Don't you want to wait for your brother? We can arrange for you to stay over."

"No, I have nothing to offer my brother, nor anything to gain by staying. This barbarian backwater—your barbarian backwater, gentlemen—has claimed another innocent life over a pointless and ultimately insignificant struggle. Do either of you think that, in the grand panorama of human history, any-one will care about the inevitable passing of the Palestinians or the Israelis any more than we care about the demise of the long-dead Etruscans."

"Etruscans? I don't understand."

"Precisely."

The two men looked at each other in silence, the one with the controlled calm of a trained professional, the other with calculated ferocity.

"Please, shall we go?" Hargrove clipped the question into a command. Roth, his face now more ruddy than ever, continued to stare at him for several seconds before turning to the door and exiting without looking back.

It was not until he was back in his hotel room that Hargrove let himself indulge in the feelings that were rising in him like sour vomit. His hands shook in rage and impotence as he pounded on the bed.

And what would you think, my weakling brother, if you knew what I am thinking, my thoughts of revenge? What would you say?

You would say nothing, of course, as you did so many times when we were growing up, particularly when it was I who was in the soup and you who were, in truth, to blame, particularly when you could have absolved me with no more than a word. You and your cowardly, convenient silence. I wonder, in the beginning, whether you really were so slow to learn to speak. Were you afraid to speak up, even then? Or was it all an act, part of some plan, to become the pampered favorite, which, indeed, you were. For me: the marching orders, the expectations, and the demands; for you: the love, the ready forgiveness, the generosity. It was I who was sent away to public school, you who were tutored at home. I burnt the midnight oil while you coasted on the inheritance, until that was gone, and then on your wife's wealth, until she was gone. You always had it easy and did so poorly, while I got nothing and did so well. How I hated you and hate you still.

He unclenched his fists, straightened his long fingers, and reached over to the conference program resting on the nightstand. Three more days of this nonsense, he thought, these stupid academic games. I am so tired of them, the posturing, the play acting, the simulations, the massively moronic simulations, as if they had no connection to reality. He nodded as if counting. Three more days.

12

Karl spent the afternoon slipping in and out of sessions with topics of little or no interest to him in the vain hope of tracking down the elusive Rajid. At the end-of-day reception, he picked up a glass of the nondescript but quite drinkable wine they were serving, the proud product of some nearby boutique winery in the Sharon Plain. Not bad, he thought, taking a sip. Kosher wine was clearly not what it used to be. Thank God—and thank all the immigrants who had known the better stuff before they landed here, he thought. Reflexively he muttered a quick *bracha*, then laughed silently. You, he said to himself, are becoming observant in your own odd fashion. He laughed again, this time aloud.

Glass in hand, he began to drift slowly around the room

among the small knots of attendees who stood or sat, sipping wine, noshing, and schmoozing. From the tasseled ones with *tzitzit* peeking out from under their suit coats and from those crowded in at the few small tables or standing around empty handed, Karl estimated that perhaps as much as a quarter of the group in the room were observant Jews.

"Jews don't eat standing up," he had once been told pointedly by an Orthodox colleague, a reporter for the newspaper *Haaretz*. Karl had continued to munch on the nachos from his plate as he stood, watching and waiting for what he could sense was a pending punch line. "Animals do," the man had finished on a perfect downbeat.

"So true. That's me," Karl had said, smacking his lips as he walked away. "Just your basic human animal, I am," he added over his shoulder.

He had been tempted to stay and regale the pious jerk with a story about his friend Ari Goldstein, with whom he had grown up in Michigan, one of the handful of Jewish kids he knew in the small Upper Peninsula town and a frequent uninvited but welcome guest for Sunday morning breakfast of bacon and eggs and sweet rolls at the Lustig house.

"Jews don't eat pork," Ari had once told him in a seriously conspiratorial tone as he waved a crisp rasher. "But we do eat bacon," he finished before taking a bite with evident relish. The limits of Ari's unorthodoxy had been tested later one year when Karl's mother had invited him to stay for Easter dinner. Karl had tried to explain to his technically adept but socially inept parents, both engineers of some standing in the community, that Ari was Jewish. They protested, saying that Jesus was a Jew, and Ari volunteered that he had no qualms about joining in a celebration about *HaMashiach*, the messiah.

106

So Ari stayed and said nothing when the traditional Easter ham was served that afternoon. After a few bites, though, he excused himself and hurried to the bathroom, where he vomited. The irony had not escaped the young Karl, who knew that Ari was otherwise no more an observant Jew than Karl's churchless parents were believing Christians. Yet within all of them lived a visceral virtue, a conditioned or congenital impulse that seemed to override the conscious choices of the skeptical mind. Ari had then successfully excused and extricated himself, managing a fairly smooth job of it, at least for a mere schoolboy, by making a show of feeling his stomach and his forehead before musing about some gastrointestinal virus that must be going around. But Karl knew.

And Karl knew now that he still had not learned the art of social subtlety that the preteen Ari had demonstrated so many decades earlier. Karl's wisecracking treatment of the journalist had ultimately cost him, and the trickle of requests for comments or contributions to the newspaper's website had quickly dwindled to nothing.

Karl once again scanned the crowd at the reception and finally spotted a new face that might belong to someone named Rajid. The man had skin the color of buttered toast. Racial profiling has its uses, Karl thought, as long as you keep it in your head. This man was talking to Hargrove, however. Karl cursed, then thought again. It afforded him a perfect excuse.

As he approached the pair, their conversation suddenly ceased. "Please forgive me for interrupting," he said to Hargrove, "but I did want to apologize sincerely for my somewhat boorish assault this morning."

Hargrove, perhaps already softened by the wine and hors d'oeuvres, smiled and said, "No need. You, sir, are hardly responsible for my customary contempt toward journalists. It is an entirely occupational prejudice, and no personal offense is intended."

"None taken. And I was certainly out of line to presume to comment on your writing. We are both writers, true, but I suspect we are writing in opposite directions. My work has always been all about simplifying, about distilling the complicated world of technology down into an essence that is straightforward and understandable, sometimes even interesting, if and when that is possible. You are a novelist, something I have only aspired to be. As I see it, full-length fiction is all about elaboration, complicating things to keep the reader engaged and guessing, always turning the page or eagerly awaiting the next volume. Am I right?"

Hargrove nodded slightly, a nod of controlled agreement although he said nothing.

"And you sir," Karl said, turning to Hargrove's darker-skinned companion. "I hope you bear no ill will toward those of us of the journalistic persuasion. Hello and welcome," he said, extending his hand. "I am Karl Lustig, iTech Weekly. And you are," he bent to study the man's badge. "Dr. Roger Gupta," he read slowly, "affiliation unspecified. Incognito, eh? Or quasi-incognito. Charmed, Doctor Gupta."

"Just Roger, will do. That's what I usually go by, not Doctor anything. Ministry of Science and Technology, India. That's what was left off my badge."

"Roger it is, then. And you have an interest in massively concurrent computation? Or is it medieval literature?" He winked at Hargrove, who was suddenly and quite evidently uncomfortable. A young woman offering a tray of small pastries gave them all a momentary distraction, which Hargrove took as an opportunity to slip away into the crowd. Gupta craned his neck to see where the older man was headed.

"Now I am sorry," Karl said. "I seem to have interrupted something."

"No, no. We ... we only just met. Other than a shared appreciation for excursions on the canals of England, I doubt that we have much in common. I studied at the London School of Economics, you see, after moving from chemical engineering into science and technology management."

"London School? Fascinating. Quite a change, from a land with a little too much sun to one with none, eh? What led you in that direction, Roger? And, I must say, you certainly have an interesting combination of talents to do both engineering and management."

Roger smiled modestly and began to tell a cocktail-party version of his life story, his work in process control and plant management, and his views on the future of industrial robotics. Karl feigned interest as he kept scanning the crowd in search of someone named Rajid, but without luck.

The moon had already risen high over Haifa by the time Karl trudged back across the Technion campus toward his car. He took a wild chance of still catching Lev in his office, but was not terribly surprised when he got an answer with his first call.

"Shoot," said Lev.

"Nothing. Got stuck with an Indian named Roger Gupta and still haven't found your Rajid."

"All right then. Keep looking and keep us posted."

"Roger willco, over and out," Karl said as he disconnected. *I always have wanted to say that,* he thought, *and it certainly seems appropriate. Under the circumstances.*

In Tel Aviv, Lev turned from the phone to Anat. "So, you heard. We have nothing, bupkis."

"What do you think we should do?"

"Damned if I know. Why don't you check out my aunt. She goes by Novikova, Russian style. Devorah Novikova. She's old fashioned, never married, lives in Florida now, a prime bloody suspect on multiple counts. That's about as good as anything I can think of."

Anat stood to go, then turned and put her hand on Lev's shoulder. It was the most intimacy she had ever dared. He looked up at her, then at her hand. She took it away.

"I'll check out this Gupta chap. Sounds Indian, like our Rajid Bannerjee. Who knows."

"All right. Keep digging. Pyotr is working the Palestinian angle. I'm not so sure about that. Why would Islamists target a holy site of Islam? He argues that most Palestinian radicals are political rather than Islamic zealots, but ..." He stood and started pacing. "And then we have our Egyptian ghost, Hamadi el-Masri, if that is the Hamadi we are hearing about. This whole business is all shadows and speculations. We are just guessing, feeling around for phantoms in the dark. And I am wondering how much time we have in which to grasp something real, to guess right. When is the conference over, Anat?"

"End of the week. But here is an interesting bit. Bannerjee's visa application has him staying for three weeks of touring after the conference. Maybe we have time, maybe not."

Lev nodded, then put his fist to his chin. He followed her with his eyes as she walked to the door and turned, her mouth open as if to speak, but she said nothing. She held his eyes for a slow three count before heading down the hall.

What is it with these women, he thought. Rahel, Anat, that skinny young techie who works for Shimon. What do they see? I'm too old to change, ladies, a hopeless case. Isn't it obvious?

He logged off and shut down his computer. At the door, he scanned the room for a moment before turning off the lights, as if looking for something that wasn't there. It was never there, he knew, any more than it would be at the apartment when he got home. His father would have understood, of course. His father had managed somehow, managed his two marriages, the one to his wife, the other to the Institute.

"Abba, I miss you," he said aloud, in a near whisper. "You taught me so much: tradecraft, logic, how to use my head and to trust my guts, how to work the channels and how to work the streets. You just never taught me much of anything about how to live." He flicked the switch and quickly wiped his eyes in the dark before turning into the hall.

This time there was a longer message posted, a bulletin long enough to be almost visible. "All the necessary material has been delivered on schedule. Manufacturing is completed. Systems are ready for deployment. All subsystems checked. Process on schedule. Reminder: avoid contact in person. Stick to channels. Stay on plan."

13

Unable to sleep, Lev was already back in his office before the others began to arrive early the next morning. He was immersed in puzzling out how to set up some new filter parameters on Gesher Tsar when Anat danced in to his office and put a folder down right on top of his keyboard.

"Hey. Don't do that," he protested. "So, what is this that is so important?" He opened the folder as she stood grinning at him.

"We found him. Your buddy was talking with him last night," she told him. "The visa application was from Rajid Bannerjee, just as we told him, but his passport carries an AKA of Gupta, his mother's name. Among friends and colleagues, he is called Roger. So Roger Gupta equals Rajid Bannerjee. Maybe we should talk again to your *extra* special agent Karl," she teased. "What do you think?"

Lev reached for his phone and keyed in the all-too-familiar number. He quickly filled Karl in on the gist of what Anat had found.

"So, tell us, what exactly did you learn from your chat with Roger the Rajid? Anything that might help us understand what the hell is going down?"

"Well, I didn't exactly pump him," Karl said defensively. "I had no way of knowing who I was talking with. And he's Indian, not Arab, which threw me off. I was looking for a Palestinian or maybe a Lebanese, someone like that. Anyway, this guy says he had unused travel for the fiscal year and decided Israel was a nice place to visit that he had never seen before. He was a chemical engineer specializing in process control before getting an economics degree. Comes from an old family in Mumbai. Likes cats. Doesn't drink. What else do you want to know?"

Lev flipped through the documents in Anat's folder.

"Any idea why he is lying?"

"What?"

"According to customs and immigration records, this is his third time in Israel, although it has been a long time since his last visit. He actually has an adjunct appointment at Hebrew University in Jerusalem. And did he mention that he worked with India's department of atomic energy."

"Hey, if you have all this, what do you need me for. Obviously, you're better at this espionage stuff than I am. I'm just a journalist, and a poser at that."

"Don't get bent, Karl. We didn't have this information last

night. My ... my colleague just pieced it together this morning. Just tell me what you know. Did you see him talk with anyone besides you?"

"Yes. When I met him, he seemed to be hot into it with Clarkson Hargrove, you know, the British author, writes young adult fantasies, almost as big as J. K. Rowling but not nearly as rich. Then again, nobody is as rich as Rowling. Hargrove is something of a self-important prick, but then I suppose he's earned the right. Anyway, he and Gupta just met. Or so they said. And it's hard to see where a novelist and professor of lit crit, or whatever it was he was going on about, would fit into this business."

"We'll see. We'll follow up on Hargrove, but you may be right, there may be nothing to it. Just keep running into Roger the Rajid and schmoozing with him without making him too suspicious. And particularly note anyone he talks with. If you can readily keep tags on this Hargrove, too, that might also be useful, although Bannerjee/Gupta is the main concern at this point.

"In any case, this is a good start, Karl. See what you can learn today. We'll talk again later." He hung up and turned to Anat. "Okay, now we are getting somewhere. Let's just assume for the moment that talking with Hargrove was not an accident, that there is some reason for them both to be at this conference now and to happen to be talking. All that assumes that we have the right Rajid. Or maybe it's not about those two at all but about somebody else, somebody they both know. Let's see if we can find anyone having any connection with Bannerjee and Hargrove."

Anat playfully pushed him aside and started typing on his computer. "Let someone who knows how to formulate search parameters do it," she said. They watched as the screen filled with cross references. "Here's at least one name that comes up at the Technion, although she's not registered at the conference. Felicity Gold." Anat clicked on a green triangle to bring up more detail. "Okay, Gold is on the maths faculty at the Technion." She nodded and mumbled little "yadda-yaddas" as she scanned down the display. "Okay, here's something. Seems she was a graduate student at the university in England where Hargrove now holds an endowed chair. And, bingo! She and Bannerjee co-authored a professional paper a few years back: 'Cellular simulation of high-acceleration aerosol dispersion patterns.' A conference on supercomputing in Mumbai. Seems there's a PDF copy of the paper already on file in our archives, so it must have interested somebody here at some point. Hmmm, the record shows it was posted by our very own Pyotr Abramovitch. I'll get hard copy of the paper and ping him." She clicked to print out a copy of the file, then sent a quick query to Pyotr. "Most of Gold's work seems to have been in high-reliability computing for safety-critical applications."

"Safety-critical? Like what?"

"Air traffic control, nuclear power plants, that sort of thing."

"Did you say nuclear? Do we have a dossier on her."

"Hmmm. Not yet, it seems, but I can tell you from what we do have here that she's an Israeli citizen, not born here, but she made *aliyah* when she was twenty-four. Actually, now I remember hearing about her at University. Yes, I recognize this early paper of hers. So, she is *that* Gold. The Gold Standard is one of those computer science shibboleths."

"Gold Standard?"

"It's a mathematical algorithm she devised for super high-reliability computation based on triple redundancy. It's a technique she invented for combining three independent computations to get extremely reliable results. It has become the standard of reference for reliable computation, hence, The Gold Standard."

"Let's go back to Hargrove. Anything useful in customs and immigration records?"

She flipped to another screen. "He's from the UK. British tourists don't need visas in advance, so all we have is an entry flag in the record. He arrived ten days ago. And he's been here before, a regular, it seems, nearly every year for about the last decade."

"What about when he landed? He had to fill out an entry form. Can we get that, whatever he said on entry?"

"It's not in the system because that stuff is all still just on paper, but I'll see what I can get from the customs and immigration people. Hang on. What was the name of that girl who was shot in Jerusalem the other day? Wasn't she a Hargrove, too?"

"Yes, I think you're right. See if there's a relationship. I'll let Karl know about our finding Professor Gold. Wait, you know what, Anat? I think I should get Rahel to find me a field agent for the Technion, a real one. With the leads multiplying and mingling, I don't think we should be so dependent on amateurs at this point." He left unceremoniously.

She followed him with her eyes as he headed down the hall to Rahel's desk. Intriguing man, she thought. Those eyes of his! He can seem so sensitive one minute, so out of reach the next. He's probably gay.

Daniel was not expecting any calls, so he let the phone ring several times before answering it. It was the front desk announcing that he had a visitor, Chesterton Hargrove. Should they send him up? Daniel almost said no, but then realized that rejection would only prompt his brother to persist until Daniel relented or there was an embarrassing scene. He did not want his brother calling him, or worse, showing up at the conference at some inopportune time. He told the desk clerk to send his brother up in fifteen minutes. There was no real reason for the delay except to express his dislike for his brother by making him wait.

True to form, his brother knocked a little less than ten minutes later. Daniel let him knock several times before putting the chain on the door and opening it only centimeters.

"I'll be with you in a minute, Izzy. Just hang on." He closed the door in his brother's face, timed one minute by his wrist watch, then fumbled with the chain for several seconds before opening the door.

"Izzy, please do come in. I had heard that you were arriving today." His brother, Chesterton Isaiah Hargrove, hated the nickname his family had given him but always felt powerless to protest. Daniel, knowing full well that his brother preferred to be called Chet, insisted on using Izzy so long as there had never been any direct protest. He was surprised, therefore, when his brother began with a protest.

"It's Chet, Daniel. You know that," he said, as he entered the room. "You have always known that." He made a half move as if to embrace his brother, but Daniel seemed not to notice, so he extended his hand instead.

Well, my little brother has discovered a spine, Daniel thought. "Yes, of course. Chet it is, then," he said, studying his brother's face while ignoring the waiting hand. "You look tired. This is … this is all so simply dreadful, I am sure. Please sit down." He gestured toward a chair in the corner of the sitting area while seating himself in the middle of the sofa, thus keeping a couple of meters between them.

Chet stared at him impassively, his lips frozen in a horizontal line that could be anything, from resentment to boredom to indifference or even misery. It had always been hard to tell with Chet.

Minutes passed as the two men looked at each other, both their heads bobbing subtly as they stretched the silence. Were it not for Daniel's prominent sideburns, each could be looking in a mirror. Daniel had often wondered how two brothers could be so alike in appearance and be so different in all other ways, how they could come from common stock and common experiences, yet choose such different trajectories with such distinctive targets. Daniel was a Tory, Chet was Labor. Daniel was a man of letters, Chet a man of leisure. Chet was married, or had been. Daniel was a man of affairs and liaisons. Chet had a daughter, or thought he did, and Daniel knew better. Chet did not know he had been cuckolded; Daniel knew which guest conductor of which orchestra was Clarissa's biological father.

Daniel broke the silence. "Her mother didn't come?"

"Agneta is in Jerusalem, at the hospital. We try not to be in the same place at the same time. We have had many years of practice at that, intended or not. You know, Danny, she wants to end it."

Daniel grimaced at the sound of his own childhood nickname. "End it? I thought the divorce was already final."

"No. Pull the plug, cut off life support. Clarissa is not yet twenty-one, so legally still a minor, and Agneta and I had joint custody, so the hospital would need both of us to agree on what to do. Agneta wants to …" He started to cry but made no sound. "She wants to kill my little girl."

Daniel was thinking that it seemed to him his brother had already accomplished that many years earlier, but instead he said aloud, "It is not like she is really alive, anymore. She—her brain, her mind, who she was—is already gone. You need to let go."

"What would you know? You have never had anyone in your life, nothing or no one you ever cared about, except your books and your writing and lording it over your fawning students and adoring fans."

Daniel started to rise, but then sat back. "You know absolutely nothing about me or my life, Izzy," he said, stressing his brother's nickname so that there could be no mistake as to intentionality. "You chose to go another route, to marry that wealthy Dane, a flake who would take care of you with her wonderful talent but who believes in séances and the tarot and endless nonsense. Now you have chosen to leave her. These are all your choices. But your daughter is dead, and you cannot choose to bring her back. You can only choose whether or not to keep a piece of meat nourished. What a waste of medical technology. What …"

"You do not call her meat!" Chet screamed. He was up from his chair and lunging at Daniel before he finished the sentence. Daniel shifted to the side, partially rose, and swept the feet from beneath his brother, who plunged awkwardly, face first, into the cushions of the sofa. So physical a response was undignified, but Daniel nevertheless relished the rush of adrenalin and felt inordinately proud as he looked down at his younger brother struggling to right himself.

"You were never a match for me, Izzy, even as boys. And

you were never any good at knowing who the enemy was. Did they tell you who shot her, who shot your daughter? It was the Israelis, Izzy. The army shot her. The Israeli army blew her brains out, to put it somewhat crudely. If you want to attack someone or something, attack the Jewish state of Israel. Make them pay. Your daughter has suffered enough, first at the hands of an inept, depressive, weak father and a screwy, brainless but mercifully mostly absent mother, and now at the hands of the Israeli military, abetted after the fact by Israeli medicine. Give them all a taste of their own medicine."

Chet pulled himself up and stood facing Daniel. "You will never understand," he said, and started for the door.

"I understand fully. The Israelis may be murderous, but at least they are not spineless. Go. Go have it out with your muddle-headed ex-wife. Let me know what you two work out and when the funeral is to be. I just might come. But now, just go."

For several minutes after the door closed behind his brother, Daniel stood without moving. He finally seated himself at the small desk in the room and opened up his laptop. He stared at the screen, then closed it again.

Nothing has changed, he thought. Life goes on.

Part Two

14

The small crowd outside the main entrance to the mall was in a festive mood, but the guards in the security detail were becoming a bit nervous. Three new stores were opening at Haifa's famous 200-store complex, the largest *kanyon,* or shopping mall, in the country. The brilliant blue electric sign over the entrance declared it, in a multicultural, multilingual play on words, to be the "Grand Kanyon." With the bottleneck created by the newly erected barrier and metal detectors at the entrance, the queue outside kept growing, as more groups of young shoppers arrived after work and the end of school.

Najat pulled her coat tighter around her against the wind coming up the hill. Without her headscarf she felt both cold and exposed, but she knew how important it was to fit in with the young Israelis around her. She was not worried; she had had lots of practice fitting in. She might even know some of the people in line, although she almost hoped there were none.

It was a good time to arrive, not too early and not too late, she thought. She glanced across the road toward a cluster of apartment buildings in the distance and wondered which was the window. She knew they were watching her, somewhere out there, ready to take over if anything went wrong. I will be all right, she thought. My father named me well. I am Najat. I am safe. She thought of her cousin, Habib, hoping he, too, would soon be safe.

The line had begun moving faster now, and she saw that she would soon be at the inspection point. An armed guard walked alongside the queue, waving people forward. She stared straight ahead as she prayed silently.

The blast, which shattered the electric sign overhead and tore a hole in the side of the building, killed seven people instantly, including the security guard beside the queue, and left many gravely wounded. What had been a happily distracted crowd of young people was suddenly transformed. Cellphones came out, and almost before the smoke had cleared, sirens could be heard approaching. Those who could, attended to the injured or started clearing rubble where it lay atop the victims. One young man cursed and kicked violently at a grisly mass lying in the gutter, the armless, headless upper torso of what moments before had been a young Arab woman. A policeman, running from inside the building, grabbed him and pulled him back.

Save for the sobs of some of the injured, the scene was strangely quiet, strangely ordered, with a fine white powder incongruously blanketing the area like a dusting of fresh snow.

Lev was breathing hard as he entered the conference room. "I just got the call. Fill me in, people" he said, as he slipped into his customary place at the head of the massive olive-wood table.

"Looks like we got our answers. A suicide bomber. Outside the Grand Kanyon in Haifa," Anat said. "Security was too good for anyone to actually get in, but there was a small crowd waiting in line outside where the bomb was detonated. Current figures are 11 dead, 28 injured. The death toll is expected to climb."

Pyotr jumped in. "Emergency personnel first on the scene reported a powdery residue around the explosion. Unfortunately, before anyone figured out what they were dealing with, the contamination had already been spread, by way of victims and survivors, throughout much of the area and into at least two hospitals.

"The initial report we have is a mixture of isotopes, primarily cesium-137. Dispersal from the explosion was not particularly effective, but nevertheless we now have some contamination over a fairly wide area. Public Health is trying to locate all emergency personnel and bystanders who were in the area and get them decontaminated as quickly as possible. The entire mall and the immediate environs are sealed off, of course. Civilian defense is supposed to issue a report shortly about the prospects for decontaminating the site. In any event, this one is going to be costly."

"It's a nightmare," said Anat. "And the media are like sharks after a seal pup; it's a feeding frenzy. The first really major incident of nuclear terrorism in the world and it happens on our soil, on our watch. It's already on the cable networks and, of course, all over the Internet. There are even videos already on YouTube. One of them, a clip that was shot with a cellphone, shows a young woman making faces at her friend holding the phone just as the suicide bomber, clearly visible in the background, detonates her charge. Both the young woman and her friend were killed in the blast, but somebody retrieved the flash card from the phone and then uploaded the video. It's pretty disturbing to watch, although the clip mercifully ends just as the blast wrecks the phone. On YouTube, already. Hard to believe. You know, sometimes I don't understand this generation."

"Okay, right," Lev said, doodling on the notepad in front of him. "Get our team working on copies of everything posted online. We absolutely should have put this one together ahead of time. We could see all the dots, we just didn't connect them. Al Aqsa plus dirty bombs equals dirty suicide bombers. This is a major escalation, a new front in the terrorist war. And the answer was right in front of us, the warning signs flashing in our faces like some Internet banner ad, but we ignored them and wasted our time chasing academics at some conference at the Technion."

"Wait, *Neve Sha'anan*, the district where the Kanyon is," Pyotr interrupted. "Isn't that not far from the Technion?"

"A couple of kilometers, maybe," Anat answered. "You think there could still be a connection?"

Lev shook his head vigorously from side to side. "Forget it. This is plain old Palestinian martyrs, only now they have a shiny new weapon, one that glows in the dark. How they ever got into that part of Haifa, I don't know, but we had better figure out soon. And if what we are piecing together about that

Bulgarian deal is right, a lot more of the same could be coming our way. We better find the rest of the radioactive stash before it finds us.

"I'm going to touch base with Shin Bet. You all work Gesher Tsar for whatever you can get. There will have to be some chatter about this." He pushed back from the table and stood. For a moment he looked as if he were trying to think of something to say, then he stared into the distance and slowly crumpled, hitting his head on the edge of the table as he fell.

It was time for the Sage to post, an unsigned one-word message: Fucked.

15

If you don't mind the Anglo-Saxon," the Wizard said to the Sage, "you look like shit." She did her best to look as if she were not talking to him, just someone standing around outside the same room, as if both were waiting for a meeting to let out.

"I feel like shit," he said, talking into space as if she were not there. "If you've been reading the papers here you know about the shooting. She was just a poor student on holidays from uni. The bloody bastards killed her. A goddamned fire fight, would you believe? In Jerusalem. Stupid, bloody stupid. She got a bullet through her brain. Her brain. And now, now this.

"A pox, a pox I say, a pox on all of them." He took a deep

puff on his cigar and began to move away just as someone entered the hallway and started toward them. "Channels, goddamnit, channels," he whispered as he strode down the deserted corridor.

She caught up with him just as the Wonk rounded the corner and almost ran into them. He was obviously perplexed, not sure whether to stop or continue on by. The Sage blew a cloud of cigar smoke that caught him in the face. He stopped and coughed uncontrollably.

The Sage leaned a shoulder against the wall for a moment, then stood again, ramrod straight, and took another quick draw on his cigar. "We have work to do. Do you realize what happened yesterday?" he said, squeezing the words between clenched teeth. "Gazumped by some goddamned girl from the slums of the West Bank. Security will be trebled. We'll never be able to finish. And we can't wait, either. Give them enough time, and they will find the lab, everything. It's only a matter of time.

"What kind of a network did you put together, my so-called Wonk? Bloody freelancers? Independents? Do we have any idea how many terabecquerels were wasted by last night's little ... demonstration?"

"Maybe we should call it off," the Wizard said, turning to face the two men. "If the plan is compromised, it's compromised. And I'm not completely sure that we had the right plan in the first place. Do we even know how much was diverted by the ... the delivery service?"

"No," the Sage spoke through a cloud of smoke. "At this moment we know nothing. But you can bet the same is not true of the intelligence community. They are no doubt already sniffing every goddamned alley from here to Gaza, looking for anything that scintillates."

"Which is why the lab is where it is," the Wonk scolded.

"All right. We do nothing until we see what happens next. If necessary, we postpone the project, but not by much. A week, maybe ten days. Every extra day multiplies the risk. I am starting to wish I had never listened to you, my lovely Wizard. Wizard, indeed. More threads means more loose threads. It's like a knitted jumper, pull one loop and everything unravels."

She smiled up at him, incongruously. "You have one shot, no rehearsals. When everything depends on successful execution, you arrange the series for maximum probability of success. Remember, this is my domain. Stick to your hobbies, darling. The time for them will come." She placed a hand flat against his chest in a gesture that could be either one of affection or of rejection. He glanced down to where it rested, and she withdrew it while letting her fingers slide provocatively down his jacket.

The Wonk shook his head as if trying to clear the smoke from it. "I'll post an 'on-hold' message through the site. I'll also ask for each team to report what they have in inventory so we can estimate how much was diverted."

"Separate postings," the Wizard added. "Remember, the longer the message the easier it is to see it."

"I know, I know," he said impatiently. "Look, we have all talked for too long. The next session is about to begin and you have to get back to your grad students. No more face-to-face. That's why we set up the channels, right?"

The Sage frowned and said, "Right. Enough tête-à-tête. Use the channels." He turned abruptly and walked away at his usual long-legged pace, a clip his devoted graduate students had dubbed casual haste.

Karl inched his way along the dessert buffet, looking around, scanning the luncheon crowd. He had seen neither Hargrove nor Bannerjee all morning. From across the way, Karl noted a woman just entering the room from one corridor, then turning immediately toward another across the room. I know her, he thought. On impulse, he set down his plate, estimated his trajectory, and tried to look casual as he hurried to intercept her.

He smiled broadly as he approached. "No badge?" he said. "I would have thought a conference like this in your own backyard would be right up your alley, Professor Gold. Felicity Gold, right? I recognized you from the faculty home pages." He introduced himself as she continued to walk briskly down the corridor.

"I'm far too busy teaching and supervising research this semester to attend conferences," she said, "even ones right on my own campus. Plus, I am finishing writing a textbook—or trying to, at least. Frankly, there are just too many academic conferences these days. The old dictum of publish or perish has been transmuted into the curse to confer or collapse. The only upside is economic: the booming conference industry created in the process. And then there are all those phony multi-conferences that serve one and only one purpose: to pack CVs. One more entry in your résumé. And what do we make of all those damned email solicitations, the hokey CFPs? 'Your paper has already been accepted.' Garbage. As if we didn't have enough spam."

She slowed down. "Wait. I do know you. I recognize you from the headshot on the banner of your blog. I have actually read some of your stuff online. Isn't distributed supercomputing a bit off the beaten path for you?"

"Truth? Yes, but I live here in Haifa, and a client picked up my registration fee, so I thought I might broaden my horizons. Actually, there are a lot of interesting people here, even if the sessions are a bit dry. For instance, I got to meet one of my son's literary heroes, Clarkson Hargrove. Do you know him?"

"Not really. Is he here? I should have to look him up and say hello. I did once help him solve a programming problem when I was studying in England."

Karl frowned. "Oh, I must be mixed up. I thought you were one of his graduate students, before you moved from philosophy to computer science."

She turned her head to the side and looked at him askance. "Well, yes. That, too, but it was another career and a long time ago. I haven't even seen him since I returned to Israel. But how is it ... why is it you know this?"

"I'm a journalist, not by training, but by temperament. Plus, it buys the groceries. I was just doing my homework. Actually, it was my son's doing. He can't believe I have personally talked with *the* Clarkson Daniel Hargrove. He regaled me with Hargrove's entire life story, including his relationships—alleged relationships we journalists would have to say— with certain grad students, most notably the notable Dr. Felicity Gold. Oh, don't be surprised. Or offended. Everything but everything is on the Web. In fact, that last little factoid is right straight out of your Wikipedia bio, in case you were wondering. Hardly anything we do is truly private anymore."

"Clearly, I have been leading a sheltered, limited life buried in my algorithmic research here. I had no idea. And what would I find in the Wikipedia about you?"

"Not much, I'm afraid. In fact, my current entry, which

was actually started by my publisher, is designated a 'stub,' with one of those generic pleas for further work to bring it up to proper Wikipedian standards. There are some benefits to relative obscurity." He grinned at her.

"I can see that. I suppose once the *djinn* are out of the biographical bottle, there is no putting them back. I imagine I should Google myself more often and check out that Wikipedia entry to see what dirt is being dished about me."

"Well, if you check the 'talk' pages, you will find that there are even those who question crediting you with invention of the Gold Standard, which some are claiming is actually nothing more than a rehash of work anticipated way back in the 1970s by Habermann."

She raised her eyebrows. "Oh, really? I can see I do not follow these semi-public spats closely enough. Of course, I drew on Habermann's work, and Knuth's, and Karp's, and ... Well, we all stand on the shoulders of giants, right? But the algorithmic reliability metrics, the measurement theory, that was original, all mine. I ..." She suddenly stopped. "I am sorry. This can hardly be of interest to you, but attribution is so vital to us academics. I'm afraid we take it entirely too seriously."

"Not a problem. As a writer, I do understand. I hate it when other bloggers cut-and-paste my stuff without a link or even a thank you. Of course, I have never so much as invented or discovered anything and am unlikely to ever have anything named after me."

"Perhaps you are too modest. But, really, I do have a class to teach. My young students, who absolutely believe me when I claim credit for the Gold Standard, will be only too happy to provide me with the ego boost that those anonymous Wikipedian weasels would deny me. To be candid, I think the rubbish is probably all due to that damned Welshman, Blayney, who has been sullying my reputation every chance he can get ever since he was passed up for my endowed chair here at the Technion. He wishes he were half the man I am." She beamed at Karl, then hurried off.

Karl whistled softly as he strolled back toward the main hall.

There was a flurry of postings, from the Wonk and from some of the more peripheral contributors, as well as several from the Wizard. The Sage was too upset to post a long message, so he expressed his pique with a picture, a detail from a Hieronymus Bosch painting that struck him as singularly fitting, that and a repeat of his earlier one-word declaration.

16

Anat pushed the curtain aside, pulled a chair over beside the bed, sat down, and took his hand. "How are you doing, Lev?" she asked.

Lev opened his mouth and struggled to speak, but for some reason he couldn't think of how to say the words. "Ahhh," he said. This sucks, he thought. What the fuck is wrong with me? He tried again to speak, but not even a sound came out.

"That good? Well, I am glad to hear it." She scanned the private room with its stylishly understated furnishings and nodded approvingly. "Pretty posh. I finally get to see how the other side lives.

"Oh, in case you haven't been briefed, you have had an ischemic event, as the doctors say. A stroke, to the rest of the world. Not a real big one, according to the specialist I spoke with, but it hit part of the speech area resulting in aphasia, so it may take you a while to learn to talk again. This is a relief to many of us at the office who have always found your morning briefings much too long-winded." She winked, then pulled a small writing tablet from her pocket. "Here, see if you can still write. I'll take it with me and shred it later, so feel free to write absolutely anything."

He took the pad from her and extracted the pen from the vinyl sleeve on the side. Where do I start, he thought, then wrote one word on the pad and turned it to show Anat. "Kanyon?" it said.

"The bomber has been identified. Najat Bishara. How is that for a name? Neither 'safe' nor 'good news' by my reckoning. Jewish by birth, believe it or not, but raised by her Isareli Arab father after the mother died. She was living in Haifa and had been a student at the Technion for a while. Somewhere along the line she became radicalized, most likely by her uncle, a known Palestinian activist although not until now a suspected terrorist. But she was just not at all anyone who would have come up on our radar.

"She has other relatives, Palestinian, in the West Bank. In fact, she may be related to one of the boys involved in the most recent radiation poisoning. We are turning their neighborhood inside out with the full cooperation of the Palestinian Authority, now that the whole thing has been blown open by the Haifa attack. Because it's domestic, Shin Bet has the lead and is working with the Authority, but we are still involved, of course, because of the international angle. We should have details from the field soon. It appears that everyone involved in the caper was quite sloppy with the stuff. We have found trace amounts on several buses and at the girl's Haifa apartment."

Lev scribbled again on his pad. "Composition?"

"They confirmed it's a mix of radioisotopes, a strange mess, possibly deliberately concocted to complicate decontamination. Some of it is relatively short half-life and particularly hot, others, like the cesium, will be less hot but for a long time. The woman had a radioactive waste dump strapped around her waist. It could have been a lot worse, but apparently the bomb makers didn't know how to disperse the powder very effectively. Still, a lot of people are getting radiation sickness. We may even lose most of the people who were at the site of the bombing, including some of the first responders. It is a mess. We need to be better prepared next time."

Lev tried to say something, then remembered the pad and wrote, "More? Others?"

"Nobody is claiming credit for the bombing yet, but it is clear this woman did not work alone. She may not have known all the details, but someone knew exactly what they had, even if they didn't know how to use it to maximum effect. I don't think we've heard the last of them, though. It's still very much back-of-the-envelope, but we have estimates from the field based on the flood of cash showing up in Bulgaria that suggest that enough material may have been moved for dozens of devices like the one used in the Kanyon operation. Shin Bet is interrogating a Palestinian man whose house may have been a way station for some of the stuff. No word yet on what they learned. Should I push them to share?"

Lev nodded. This is going to be tricky, he thought, then quickly scribbled, "Give everything we have. Offer help. Request nothing. Yadin will come through."

"I understand." She squeezed his hand. "I am beginning to

rather enjoy this sort of conversation. I can get more than just an occasional word in now and then. But I need to get back. We're short-handed at the office. Seems the boss hit his head on a conference table." She grinned as she backed away and slowly let go of his hand.

One more thing, he thought, as he grunted and gestured for the pad and pen again.

"You still have it," she said. "I forgot to take it back. Ah, here it is." She picked it up from the bed and placed it in his hands.

He quickly wrote, "Keep Lustig, follow conference, Dome. Hunch all related. You're lead now." You can handle it, he thought.

She took the pad from him and said, "Okay, boss. Don't worry. Just get better." As she turned away and headed for the door, she silently mouthed the words that bubbled up, unbidden: "I love you."

Outside the room she leaned back against the wall. Seeing him like that, so vulnerable, had hit her hard and brought all her feelings right up to the surface. Yes, she had wanted to someday head the team, but not like this. Pull yourself together, she thought. Just remember, the important thing is not to be afraid.

17

The moment Karl closed the apartment door behind him, Shira snapped at him. "Damn it, Karl, what are you involved with? What have you gotten us mixed up in."

"What are you talking about?" he said, hanging his cap and jacket on adjacent pegs by the door and adjusting the jacket so that the sleeves hung evenly. He carefully removed his shoes and lined them up directly beneath the pegs before pulling on his slippers.

She swung at him with the newspaper in her hand. "What am I talking about? I'm talking about nuclear terrorism. The goddamned dirty bomb at the mall, what else? Or are you so busy buzzing around with your own new cyberspace crowd that you have lost touch with reality?"

Karl dumbly shook his head. "I've been at the conference, working, working for Lev. I need to get in touch with him, too, but haven't been able to raise him at his office. And, of course, I know about the suicide bomber. I've just been a little too busy to pick up a paper. I figured I would catch the news when I got here." He lifted the paper from her hands and opened it. "Caught it! Like I said." He grinned broadly, then started reading. After a quick scan of the front page, he looked up at her.

"I don't think this has anything to do with what Lev is working on. That group ... Shit, I can't talk about it, you know that."

"Then shit right back to you. I don't want it this way. I had all those years with Migdal and that look and that voice that said we couldn't talk about it. I want to know what's going on. If you are going to put us all at risk, I want to be part of it. I don't like being in the dark, and I don't like being out of control."

"Well, I for one can testify to that, my control-freak darling," he said, ducking an imaginary blow that never came.

"I am serious," she barked at him. "If you are going to do this, then I am going to do it with you. I do not care for the word 'no.' I thought you learned that the time when you didn't want me to go with you to Boston."

"I learned that you are a determined, stubborn, wonderful woman. Yes."

"You didn't say clever. A determined, stubborn, wonderful, clever woman. You could add beautiful. And useful. Remember that, too. Very useful. I helped you with the puzzle of that mezuzah. Or did you conveniently forget?" She grabbed the newspaper back from him and raised it like a hatchet.

"Never argue with a woman who threatens with lethal print media," he said. "Okay, I'll ask Lev. As soon as I can get through to him."

She reached down for his backpack where he had balanced it against his leg and shoved it into his hands. "Then do it. Email him now. Or use whatever communication channel you amateur intelligence operatives prefer to use these days. Just do it."

"Twitter." he said. "We use Twitter to broadcast instant short messages to the world, knowing that they'll be lost in the noise of terabytes of tweets, the never-ending nonsense from all the twits who think themselves to be the very center of the Internet universe, their every move and thought of interest to the entire planet." He paused. "Okay, I can see you are not amused. So, just let me log on and see if I can get a secure message through."

He pulled out his laptop, set it up on the kitchen table, drafted an encrypted email, and sent it off to Lev. As he skimmed through the backlog of messages in his inbox, the laptop pinged, announcing an incoming encrypted message. He entered his private key to open it.

Karl,

I work with Lev. He is in hospital after suffering a mild stroke that has left him unable to talk. I am handling his assets. Talk to me. What do you have? I'll ask him about adding Shira to the list when I see him tomorrow.

Anat Dorfman

Acting Chief, Tech Ops

"Lev is in the hospital," Karl said to Shira. "He's okay, I guess, but this woman, Anat Dorfman, is taking over for him. We'll have to wait for a decision tomorrow. Meanwhile I have to send in a report. I'm sorry, but you'll just have to sit tight until we can get the okay."

"Remember, I don't do 'sit tight.' I'll just have to start working on my own." She headed down the stairs to her studio and returned a few minutes later with her own laptop, which she opened on the kitchen table opposite Karl. She smiled at him as it booted up.

Twenty minutes later, as Karl was finishing the draft of his report for Mossad, she closed her laptop and smiled across at him.

"Some terrorist network is planning an assault on *Har HaBayit*."

"How do you know? How do you know about the Temple Mount?"

"I just asked our son, he told me about the coordinates, and then I put two and two together."

"Bini? Bini broke confidence to tell you that? Oh, great. This is just great."

"Don't be too hard on him. I don't think a twelve-year-old boy realizes that 'do not talk with anyone' extends to his mother."

"And you used email?"

"Encrypted, PGP. I'm no dummy."

"I am going to have to tell Lev. Or this Dorfman person."

"Okay, but wait until after you get Lev's decision about whether I am on the job, too. If he says yes, it's all moot anyway."

"All right, all right. But back up a bit. This theory about a terrorist network attacking the Dome of the Rock just makes no sense. Who would do that? The area is sacred to everyone: Jews, Muslims, Christians."

"That, oh brilliant husband, is not quite everyone. What about the Buddhists, the Baptists, and the Jains."

"'Universal Soldier,'" he said quickly, "by yet another underappreciated Canadian singer-songwriter, Buffy Sainte-Marie." Shira scowled at him with a look of mixed confusion and annoyance. "How quickly we forget the song that helped bring us together. Cory Hart, 'Sun Glasses at Night.' And now we have 'Universal Soldier,' a classic, even if a bit overwrought. You were quoting—or misquoting—a sixties folksong. It would have to be the Buddhists, the Baptists, and the Jews—or better, the Hindus, the atheists, and the Jains. Still, what would anyone of any persuasion stand to gain? They would be hated and hunted by everyone."

"No one has to gain anything, dear. Terrorism is not rational and is seldom about rational gain. It's about spreading terror. Besides, I only report the news, I don't make it."

"Hang on there, reporting the news, are you now? Who's the darned reporter here? Remember, I'm the journalist. You, my darling, are a silversmith, an artist who is once again swimming out of her depth."

"I never worry about the depth of the water I swim in, as long as I'm on top of it. And I am a far better swimmer than you, my darling, as I proved when we went swimming at Ga'ash," she said, referring to an incident in which Karl had been distracted and ended up drifting out with the tide.

"Now don't start," Karl protested, thinking about the embarrassment of being hauled back to shore by his young wife. "And please stick to the subject. You think some terrorists are going to try to blow up the Dome of the Rock?"

"Yes. It could even be our people. We, too, have our extremists."

Karl nodded. "That is true, so sadly true. But let's wait until we hear from Lev before we construct any more wildly speculative scenarios."

"My scenarios are speculative but not wild," she said, playfully kicking him under the table.

With a carefully posed mask of exaggerated pain on his face, he reached down to grab at his shin. She kicked him again.

18

Rabbi Menachem hid his fear behind fury. "Why are you holding me? Why are you questioning me? I'm an Israeli citizen and an Orthodox Rabbi. You have no right to do this without charges. What are the charges? You must tell me the charges. By what authority are you holding me?" He continued, repeating with variations the same questions and complaints, as if it were a chant from the liturgy.

Rafi Yadin watched from the corner as the two Shabak interrogators sat in ominous silence, waiting for the outburst to subside. He knew the reputation of his own service, but had somehow managed thus far to avoid ever participating directly in an interrogation. He was not sure what he would be called on to witness, but he dared not protest or excuse himself. It was more than a matter of saving face; it was a matter of survival within the complex pecking order of Shin Bet. When the Rabbi finally stopped, the bigger of the two men glanced toward Rafi before standing and walking slowly toward the Rabbi.

"You are one of the Temple Mount Faithful, are you not, Rabbi?"

"You know very well who I am and about the organization I helped found. We are no longer part of the Temple Mount and Eretz Yisrael Faithful Movement. You know that as well."

"Then, how do you feel about the Dome of the Rock and the Al Aqsa Mosque."

"I feel nothing about them. They are neither more nor less than abominations that should be destroyed." He stopped for a moment, appraising his opponents, wondering what they knew, what they believed, and what arguments might be persuasive. "Then, at last, the Third Temple can be built and *Ha-Meshiach* can come," he said, looking for a reaction that never arrived.

His tall antagonist stood over him and placed a foot on the Rabbi's chair. "You are Messianics, then?"

"Not in the sense most would use the term. We have more immediate concerns, though we believe with perfect faith that He will come. But first, we must restore the Temple and resume the traditional practices, all of them."

"Ritual sacrifice, you mean. Oh, yes, that would be just what modern Israel needs: slaughtering lambs and perfect heifers to appease *Adonai*, splashing their blood on the altar." He turned to his partner. "That will certainly raise our esteem among the nations, no doubt. Tell us, then, Rabbi, how you would propose to rid the Temple Mount of its Islamic abominations."

"With bulldozers. The Temple Mount Faithful tried to negotiate, to persuade the Muslims to move the Dome and the Mosque to Mecca. But the stubborn Arabs would have nothing of it. They, they want the Western Wall of the Temple buried to rid them of the repugnant presence of pious Jews davening at the site. Our site." He shook his fist at no one in particular. "There were Jews there when there was no such thing as Muslims. And there will be Jews there still when no one remembers that Muslims once walked the earth."

In the corner, Rafi could hear in his head the sound of a men's chorus trumpeting a line from *Patizaner Lidt*, the song of the partisans of World War II: "Our marching feet will thunder, 'we survive!'" He suppressed a snigger at the sentiment and the Rabbi's pugnacious style, but, as the laugh stuck in his throat, for a moment he began to feel some of the zeal expressed by the Rabbi.

"Bulldozers?" An explosion of spittle, highlighted by the harsh backlighting, sprayed across the gap between the interrogator and the Rabbi. "Why not a bomb? So much faster and far more dramatic."

"A bomb would work. It would not even have to be a very big bomb. During the Six-Day War, when we retook Jerusalem and *Har HaBayit*, Rabbi Goren is said to have suggested to the military to use a few hundred pounds of plastic explosive to settle the matter once and for all. They should have listened to him. I heard that he said he would have gladly done it himself, given the chance. I feel the same. But a bomb is unnecessary when heavy equipment will do the job. Besides, in the end, after the bomb, the rubble would still have to be bull-dozed away. No, bombs are crude and inefficient. Let the Pal-estinians use bombs. Let them blow things up, themselves in the process, if that be their preference. We do not mourn for dead Muslims. May they hasten their own departure from the world."

"Who would do this clearing of the rubble, Rabbi? Tell me, who would operate the bulldozers and the front loaders? Would you?"

"I would tear everything down brick by brick, board by board, and stone by stone with my bare hands, given the op-portunity. We should never have ceded control over the Tem-ple Mount back to the Muslims. We should have leveled it when we had the chance. Now ... now it will be more diffi-cult."

The questioning went on for several hours, returning more than once to the matter of motive and method for eliminating the Dome and the Mosque. Finally the second interrogator said, "Enough!" and directed that the Rabbi be ushered out. Once the Rabbi was gone, the interrogator looked to his part-ner and said, "Do you believe him?" and then to Rafi, "And you, do you believe him?"

Rafi shook his head and shrugged. "I'm no expert on this sort of thing. I'm your science and technology guy. But it seems plausible to me that this group could be behind a plot to attack the Dome. I would watch them closely. And check with our friends at Mossad to see if there are any similar or connect-ed international groups. Who else would be interested in seeing the Islamic sites destroyed or the Temple rebuilt?"

"Some fundamentalist Christians, you know, Evangelicals, Messianics."

"Right, we should make sure that those groups are being dogged as well. I understand there is a group of American biblical archeologists digging around under the Old City right now. What are they up to? They should be checked out and tracked, brought in for questioning."

"So, as you are saying, the usual suspects have spread. From thinking that common interests meant that none of the big three religious groups would be out to destroy their shared sacred site, now we have to consider that it could be any of them: the Palestinians wanting to make a political point and possibly pin it on the Jews, right-wing Jews wanting to clear the site to rebuild the Temple, and fundamentalist Christians wanting to set the stage for the return of their savior."

"God save us from the true believers."

"Amen selah."

Rafi frowned. "What I don't understand is this business about a dirty bomb. If you want to level a place, ordinary explosives would do just fine. Or bulldozers, if you believe the Rabbi. Why a nuclear assault?"

"Well, maybe the bomb is just a bomb, and the nuclear piece is misdirection or distraction. Maybe the operation in Haifa and this threat are unrelated. There are so many enemies out there. *Rag'shu goyim.*"

"Indeed, the Nations rage," Rafi confirmed. "We could be dealing with several unrelated groups operating in tandem, all bent on sowing disorder and destruction.

"Changing the subject, did you get anything out of the Palestinian family, the one whose house had been used as a way station for the radioactive material?"

"The house, it seems, was a stopover for a courier, who left behind a packet of the stuff. It is not clear whether he was persuaded or it was an accident, but after the two boys got sick, somebody in the community figured out what they had and word got to some hotshots in a Hamas faction. The packet was picked up and finally dropped off, as it were, at Grand Kanyon. This may have been a rogue operation or it may be the first of a planned series. We have to treat it as one of many to be better prepared next time. If there is a next time. I think *Har HaBayit* is the real worry. Or perhaps worry is not the word. Maybe *tikvah*, would be a better word. We can hope it is one target and a single terrorist group."

Rafi nodded grimly, then took his leave. He stopped just outside the building and stood, taking in deep breaths, calming himself. The interrogation had been neither bloody nor violent, and he knew it could have been both. He found himself thinking sympathetically about the Rabbi's position. Maybe this could be a good thing after all, he thought. Maybe not stopping it could be the best thing we could do. Perhaps it's time we all let go of some ancient memories and rid ourselves of masonry and mortar symbols that should have long ago lost all value and all power to divide. He recalled reading a transcript of an address Shimon Perez had once delivered in the United States, in California, in which he had said that the Middle East needed a generation of Palestinian and Israeli youth unschooled in history, a generation prepared to forget the past in order to start afresh. We need to wipe clean the slate, he thought, or perhaps the face of *Har HaBayit*. He shook himself all over and headed for his car. His cellphone started ringing just as he opened the car door.

Rabbi Menachem was strangely elated as he made his way slowly back to his office. It was not merely that the interview was over and that he had survived something that could have easily turned ugly. It was the subject matter being pursued that raised his spirits. Perhaps his old friends—or even his old enemies—among the Temple Mount Faithful were finally up to some good deeds after all. Or perhaps some deluded sect from America was busy transforming its misguided messianic fantasies into convenient reality. He didn't care. As long as the abomination atop *Har HaBayit* was destroyed, by whatever means, he would dance in the streets like a Chassid. If it were a group from among the Temple Mount Faithful, perhaps he could help. He wondered. Perhaps he should reach out and see. No. But when nothing but a pile of rubble remained, he would be among the first to line up with shovels to clear the way for the Third Temple. "*Hashem* willing, may I live to see that day," he said aloud.

Lev picked up his office phone without thinking. It was Rafi. "We think we have a lead on your Egyptian."

"Uh ... minute. Still having trouble ... speaker ..." He pressed the button for the speakerphone and looked pleadingly toward Anat.

"Rafi, hello. This is Anat Dorfman. I'm acting Chief of Technical Services for the moment, but Lev is here, too. What have you got?"

"We picked up an Egyptian engineer named Abasi when he tried to buy some fiber optics from one of our agents. He is a supplier, a very successful one, it seems. We found a veritable warehouse in his apartment, a mish-mash of high-tech gear." He read from a list: "DC motors, miniature hydraulics, controller microchips, opto-isolators, stuff that I can only guess about what it's for, except probably not for anything good, we can assume. Anyway, we grabbed his cellphone before he could dump it and found a contact entry labeled Hamadi with several numbers. The country code on one of them is 359, Bulgaria. The guy is very smart but not very sophisticated. He claimed he didn't remember what he supplied to Hamadi, but when we asked where we might find this Hamadi, he told us without blinking. Want to come along for the ride on this one? He's your target, actually."

Lev nodded to Anat. "Sure," she said. "But it would be better if we can tail him for a while. Maybe he'll lead us to others."

"Do we have the luxury of time at this point?"

"Twenty-four hours. Then you can bring him in. Okay?"

"Okay. We have to find him first, though. When does the clock start ticking? Now or when we get him under surveillance?"

"You are a stickler, Rafi," she said, laughing. "You find him, tell us, then punch the stopwatch."

This time the message was in plaintext, posted on a completely different site, one frequented by teens and preteens. Only to someone looking for it, waiting, would it have meant anything. Next to the handle "MOMZOID9" it read: "Clean your room."

19

This was the part of the work that Rajid hated most. It fell to him because he was the project manager, the one person who knew where everything was and what connected with what. Other nodes would be shut down by technicians, professionals whose only contact with the initiative was a single assignment and a contract paid in cash. But some few of the primary nodes, the most critical connections, needed to be handled personally, by Rajid.

The man, who was known by many names but to Rajid had called himself Asar, was a businessman, a merchant who mixed his many secular skills with a sectarian passion that reached a peak in his singular hatred of Jews and everything Jewish. He approached now with a smile and a frown, intermixed like honey and lemon on his face. "I was not expecting to be summoned, my friend," he said. "Is it time?"

"It is," Rajid answered. "It is time."

"Allah be praised!" He pounded a fist into his open palm as the frown smoothed and his smile broadened. "Now the Zionist swine will feel the Sword of the Prophet."

"Were you followed?" Rajid asked. The man waved a gesture of dismissal with his hand. "Are you carrying?"

"Of course," the man answered, puzzled.

Rajid held out his hand and waited. Asar slowly reached beneath his robe, his uncertainty increasing. The handgun he withdrew was nothing special but was fitted with an oversized suppressor considerably larger than the pistol itself. Amazing, thought Rajid, what you can tuck unnoticed beneath those robes. Asar paused with the gun held awkwardly in front of him until Rajid withdrew his own Glock from his belt and extended it toward the other man, who, still puzzled, took it and allowed Rajid to take his weapon.

"I would own one of these someday," he said, reverently turning the Glock over in his hands.

"Of course," Rajid said as he chambered a shell in the man's pistol. There was a sound outside, a soft rustling, and Rajid turned toward it suddenly, as if startled. Reflexively, Asar turned, too. Rajid shot him in the side of the head before he could turn back.

I cannot look them in the eyes. I cannot see their faces. Is there something wrong with me? he wondered. Am I weak in my disbelief? Or am I only human? It bothered him that he felt anything at all. It was just part of the job. It should be no harder than removing a defective actuator from a servo-mechanism or discarding a spent fluorescent tube. He did not fear for his own soul any more than he mourned for the death of the man lying at his feet. Neither had a soul, neither was more than mere matter to him, and yet it mattered somehow.

He listened without moving. The bulky silencer had done its job. No one had heard.

Rajid shivered and shook his head. He wiped the gun in his hand with a cloth from his pocket and wrapped the man's dead fingers around it. He squeezed the man's finger to fire another round into the wall opposite and leave powder residue on the hand. He next retrieved his Glock from the floor, carefully wiped the dust from it, and returned it to his belt. Then he walked back out into the chill of the moonless night. One down, two to go, he thought, as he chewed on his lip. Another shiver went down his back, and he pulled his jacket more tightly around him. With his butterscotch complexion and dressed like a Palestinian peasant, he would go unnoticed as he completed the night's work.

20

We have bodies," Anat said to the group gathered around the conference table. "We are being buried in bodies. In the course of less than thirty-six hours we have bodies turning up all over Gaza and the West Bank. We have bodies in Lebanon, in Jordan, in Bulgaria and Austria. We even have bodies in England, for God's sake. Well, one body, anyway. Don't know what to make of it. He was an Iranian with a British passport.

"Every one of these jobs is different. The victims seem to have no links, nothing in common, except that most of them were already on our watch lists, and they were all clearly taken out by professionals. There were no prints, no clues, no witnesses, just a bunch of almost simultaneous executions."

She slapped the folder she was holding down on the table and looked around. "Shin Bet is working on the ones in the West Bank, the police have two in Tel Aviv to investigate, and we're cooperating with Interpol and other agencies on the international ones, but I don't think we are going to find anything. Except maybe more bodies. Somebody is wiping the slate clean, making sure no one is left standing to talk about whatever they have been doing, pulling the plugs so we can't complete the circuit. It can mean only one thing."

Pyotr squinted and drilled her with his intense blue eyes. "But we still don't know what or who exactly we're dealing with, much less what is going to happen."

"True, but we are clearly running out of time. We have to connect the dots. We can't fail on this. We can't."

Rafi was just settling down with his coffee when his cellphone buzzed in his pocket. He put it to his ear and said, "What?"

"We've found Hamadi," the voice on the line said.

Rafi waited a moment before responding, "Super, bring him in for interrogation."

"He's dead. He was one of those taken out over the weekend. They only just now found the body in an abandoned house in the West Bank near the Wall."

"I assume you mean the separation fence, not the Western Wall. We're not Palestinians, remember; we don't call it a wall, much less *the* Wall. Just make sure nobody touches anything until I get there," he said, as he headed for the door.

The tiny, dirt-floor cottage had been a hovel even before it had been abandoned. Now shafts of sunlight from holes in the roof sliced the dusty air and carved bright lines across the floor and over the body sprawled there.

"Looks like suicide," Gila said. Gila was Rafi's right-hand woman: clever, competent, but inexperienced and inclined to premature conclusions. Her temper was almost as short as her cropped hair, and she did everything with impatient energy.

"Looks, but isn't," Rafi said, squatting to get a closer look. "This man could not have shot himself in the head with that." He pointed to the gun in the dead man's hand. "Forensics will have to confirm this, but with that suppressor on the gun, he would have to have been a contortionist to shoot himself at that angle. No, this is a somewhat amateurish attempt to make it look like suicide." He leaned over the body. "And, what have we here? Give me your torch." He took the pocket flashlight from her and held it close to the ground, casting into relief an impression in the dust. "It's smeared a little, but this is definitely the outline of a semiautomatic dropped here. From the position of the arm, it was dropped by our Hamadi, so it had to be retrieved by the assassin. Must have been his gun. No sign of a struggle, so Hamadi knew him. And they would only be here, in a spot like this, if it was an arranged meeting. They knew each other.

"Any other apparent suicides on the log over the week-end?"

"Two," she said as she flipped through papers on her clipboard.

"Okay, let's go see if we can dig up anyone or anything that connects them."

She groaned as she flipped a page on her clipboard. "One of them is another Egyptian, our engineering friend, Abasi. So they are connected and they are both dead and we can guess killed by the same wannabe assassin."

"Hmmm. Hamadi was an old pro who had been around for a long time. You don't survive in his world as long as he did by being careless, so let's assume for the moment that we aren't going to find out anything more through him. But Abasi was relatively new to the game and had a tendency to be sloppy. Let's recheck his apartment and hope that he was careless in a useful way."

When Gila and Rafi finally arrived at the apartment, the body was already gone, and a police forensics team was tagging evidence.

Rafi reached toward a box of parts on a table. "Watch it," he was told. "We want to be able to dust for prints on everything."

"I'll be careful," he said resentfully. He hated the disposable plastic gloves now in standard use by security and intelligence services, but still grabbed a couple from the dispenser box on the floor in the middle of the room and pulled them on. His hands began to sweat almost immediately.

Abasi had stashed his sundry electronics, motors, and high-tech miscellany in cardboard boxes and stacked them around the small apartment. Most bore imprints associated with their original contents: "10 count, 4N linear motors," "Avanel Avionics," "Slade Controls." Some of the original labels had been crossed out and rewritten with red or black marker in English or Arabic: "HV relays," "new opto-isolators," "large fasteners," "junk." About half the boxes also already bore yellow evidence tags.

Rafi walked around among the boxes that had been moved to the center of the room. On the back of one labeled Michigan Milling was a crossed-out word scribbled in red marker. Rafi bent to read it: "Rajid."

"Find something?" asked a plainclothes officer with a notepad.

"No, nothing," he said. "Nothing but boxes of junk." They both laughed as Rafi headed out into the hall where Gila was waiting. He turned and said, "Send me a copy of the inventory when it's complete. Okay?"

The man nodded and returned to his work.

21

"Come on in," Shira said to Anat. "Sorry to make you drive all the way up here, but the kids have found something and Bini wanted to show you in person. Actually, the truth is you are a second-choice stand-in, since he really wanted to show his Uncle Lev, but I explained to him that Lev was still recovering and you were taking over for now. How is Lev doing?"

Anat nodded her head a few times, looking for words. "He's doing fine, really, I suppose. He gets very frustrated at times, not being able to talk easily, always struggling, and yet he stubbornly insists on being back at the office fulltime. Even more than fulltime now, with all that has been going on of late. I think he is more or less oblivious to the impact he has on those around him, many of whom wonder whether he has lost more than just spoken words. I ..." She stopped herself from continuing. "Look, I don't mean to be rude, but I have a job to do, and I need to get back. I drove up as a favor to Lev, and I understand that he is like family to you, but please just tell me what you have."

Shira said nothing and made no move, but she was thinking about Lev—and Anat.

"Is something wrong?" Anat asked.

"No, nothing. Just thinking. Look, my son and his friends may have come up with something for you and Lev. Here, follow me to my son's 'office.'"

Bini was waiting for them, sitting at the computer in his bedroom. Shira looked around in amazement. She had never seen the room look so clean and well organized. She wondered where Bini had managed to stash all the stuff but then noticed a shirt sleeve peeking out from under the bed. Boys, she thought, they never change.

"Hey, come over here." Bini waved to them. "You must be Anat. Uncle Lev told me all about you. He thinks you're something special."

At a loss for words, Anat just scowled in confusion.

"That's my son!" Shira said, pointing across the room. "Gets right to the point. Even the embarrassing or personal or private point. Just don't take him too seriously."

It was Bini's turn to furl his brow in confusion. He shrugged and pointed. "Here, you can sit there on the bed. You gotta see this."

He opened a browser window and went right to Face-Folder.org. "We got the idea a few days ago when there were all these new pictures posted all of a sudden like. One of them was weird. This one, the piece of a painting, caught our attention first. Not the sort of thing you post on a photo sharing site, but it was the one next to it that turned out to be really interesting. NancyPants, that's her handle on our team, said it was a repeat, that she remembered seeing the same photo posted before by the same user. Again, not what you expect if you're sharing your pics with people. Plus, I already told Lev that we thought that many of the pictures were actually clipart rather than personal photos. You can tell. There's a certain look to clipart photos, too polished, too professional, too posed.

"Okay, so NancyPants found the match for the one on the left. Except it isn't a match. It's the same photo all right. See, side by side. But. They are not identical, not quite. When you blink them like this," he clicked a button that lined up the two pictures in the same spot and then switched back and forth between them, "well, see, you can tell they are not *exactly* the same. There's a bunch of pixels that are different, which doesn't make sense. Either they are the same photo, which would make them exactly match, or they are going to be lots different, all over, like if one had been resized or resampled or compressed or color corrected. No these are different in only a few dozen pixels, which you can see if we subtract one picture from the other." He clicked another button and the frame went black except for a few handfuls of scattered colored dots.

"They're using steganography," he announced with a dramatic flair.

Anat smiled broadly and gave Bini a pat on the shoulder. "Not bad, not bad. You kids are quite impressive. It's a message board, hidden in plain sight, right in front of us. We'll get cryptographics on it right away to crack the code."

"Oh, you don't have to do that. We were able to match up over a hundred photo pairs. Some of them were so lame, like shots of TV stars taken right off the Web. We found a lot of matches with Google Images. Some were tricky, and we had to write our own app that hooked into the Google API to find probable matches. Once we had a big enough cipher sample, we started busting the code itself. Turned out to be really simple. Each altered pixel encodes a single byte of the message, with the deltas split among the three color bytes, which we could get by comparing the original to the altered pixel. You following this?" Anat nodded convincingly and Shira smiled— she'd heard the explanation already, more than once. "Anyway it took," he paused and looked at a post-it note on his desk, "well, some real major number-crunching to crack the code."

"On this machine?" Anat asked, patting the outdated laptop on the desk.

"No, of course not. We have our own bot net that we use for computation-heavy applications like this. Couple thousand computers that are infected with a Trojan we wrote that allows us to steal cycles when they're idle. Nothing sinister like file sharing or anything, just using unused computer power that would otherwise be wasted. It's our contribution to, like, 'green' computing." He grinned. "We sucked a little more than 18,000 hours of CPU time from our slaves."

Anat kept shaking her head in disbelief. "You may not believe me, son, but we actually considered the steganography angle, messages hidden in the pictures. I even filed a work order to do the preliminary analysis on our supercomputer, but it's still in the job queue. Bureaucracy. You gotta love it."

Bini shook his head. "Man, I thought you guys at the Institute were smart. Massively parallel distributed computation beats supercomputers every time. I would have thought you people would know that. Here, save yourself some work." He handed her a CD. "There's a simple decoding routine in Java and transcripts of the first hundred or so messages we decoded, all tagged by posting handle and date. We're not experts like you guys, but it sure looks like my mom was right about the target. We still couldn't find anything about delivery mode. We can't figure how they could ever get any sizable IED past security around *Har HaBayit*. Boner said he'd use an aerial drop, a bomber, but he doesn't realize how good our air defense is here. No matter where they tried to fly in from, we'd scramble the fighters the minute they crossed the border. Whoosh, bam. The end."

Anat took the disk from him. "Thanks. Really thanks. I'll pass this on to Shimon and his gang of geniuses. I must say, I am impressed. No wonder Lev thinks so highly of you." She signaled to Shira. "Let's take a walk."

"I know what that means," said Bini.

"Good," she said. "Then keep quiet about it. This is getting very sensitive, and I would not want all your work to go to waste. I think it's time you wind down your little espionage network before something leaks. Can I trust you all to chill out or do I have to confiscate your computers. I can do it you know." She slipped a hand into her purse. "One phone call and squads from the CIA, the German federal police, and Scotland Yard will be at all your friends' houses within minutes. I mean it. We know exactly where everybody lives. So send all your pals one last message, that in the interest of national se-curity—no, make that *international* security—all activities and contacts are to be suspended until further notice. I'll let you know when you can restart. But now, your group is to go dark. Got it?"

Bini nodded.

In the stairwell leading down from the apartment, Shira turned to Anat. "Can you really do that? Do you really know where all the kids live?"

Anat laughed. "Yeah, we have tracked down the kids, but it would take days, maybe weeks, to get anything processed through channels. We are talking about a bunch of kids, here. The Americans and the Germans would both be really hard to convince there was any real security risk. Now the Brits, who have never trusted nor indulged their children, would probably take the computers with no questions asked."

Shira protested. "Hey, wait, I'm British, or at least I was raised in England, although I'm American by birth. Now I'm a dual national."

Anat smiled. "We know. Look, what I really wanted to talk about is next steps. And speaking of which, look who's here," she said, as Karl came bounding up the stairs. "You just missed the demo, Karl. Thanks to your son and his network we can now monitor their communications. And now that we can be eavesdropping, I want you to be sure to stay in constant touch. Plus, I want you to find an excuse to hang around the Technion even though the conference is over. We have a man trailing Roger the Rajid, and I want you to keep talking with Dr. Gold. I know you don't have the training, and my superiors think I'm nuts to rely so much on you, but Lev trusts you, so I do. I think. Okay? But be careful. These people, whoever they are, are playing for keeps. We already have enough dead bodies."

"Yeah, of course," Karl said as he continued up the stairs.

"For sure."

"Keep an eye on him," Anat said.

"And you do the same with Lev," Shira responded. "I know we don't know each other, and I have no right to get personal, but, well, my son gets his bluntness from his mother. Lev is important to you. And you may not realize it, but you are a lot more to him than just an able right-hand. You don't have to say anything. I'm not trying to put you in an uncomfortable spot, but I think you may be surprised yet by our Lev. He may wear the trappings of the life-long loner, but I've known him for a lot of years, and I think there may be more potential there than you think."

The two women stood looking at each other for several seconds before Anat cleared her throat. "I do need to get back to my desk," she said, starting down the stairs again.

"Remember, men are basically clueless," Shira called after her, "every last one of them, with Lev and my husband heading the list. It took Karl forever to catch on that we were meant for each other, but he did, and it worked out and was worth the effort."

Anat looked back up the stairs, wishing she could say something, the right something. In the end, her professionalism won out and she just said, "Thanks. Thanks for your help."

Shira re-entered the apartment to find Karl waiting inside the door.

"Did I miss something?" he asked.

"Probably," Shira said. "But we wouldn't expect anything less from you." She gave him a hug and a peck on the neck.

22

Anat looked around the table with everyone turned toward her, waiting. She was beginning to enjoy leading the briefings.

"The bad news is that Shin Bet either has nothing new or they're starting to clam up on us. At any rate, Yadin says that nothing significant turned up from either of the dead Egyptians, so it's up to us.

"The good news, in case somebody missed it, is that we can now track and read the messages posted on FaceFolder.org. The plaintext is still rather cryptic and indirect, but at least we are making progress. And we may be able to tell when the flag goes up.

"We're only guessing here, but we're trying to figure out

the vector for these dirty bombs. If they're going to keep trying to use suicide bombers, we may have time to start deploying some new defense measures, like radiation detectors at check points and the like. If they're really after the Dome on a short timetable, we have other and bigger problems. We may have to shut it down, which will be misread and bring the wrath of everyone splashing back in our faces, so we better have every little *nikkud* just right before we make any public announcement.

"Okay, let's start. What kind of bomb would they need to have to disperse enough radioactive dust over a sufficient area for a successful denial of access?"

"A big one," said Pyotr.

"And you are a big help. Can you be more specific?"

"Well, yes. State-of-the-art in improvised explosives right now is thermobarics, a fuel-air suspension. A relatively small charge of C4 or something similar disperses a huge cloud of ultrafine powder or even droplets of fuel oil, say. Mixed optimally with air, these are near-perfect explosives, like the fuel-air mixture in the cylinder of a well-tuned engine. Bang, it ignites and generates a huge fireball, a lot of bang for a relatively small amount of C4. More or less the same technique could be used to disperse a fine powder in the air. The powder could even be colloidal, a stable suspension in the fuel. But you would have to get the geometries and the detonation just exactly right or it wouldn't work too well. You could end up with only a small explosion and a light radioactive rain drizzling down over a limited area, maybe some fires, but not the collateral damage or dispersion from a big explosion. However, the problems are solvable. It could take quite a lot of experimentation, though. Or some hairy mathematical models run on some real computing power."

There were glances around the table. "Like distributed processors maybe?" Anat said, thinking back to her conversation with Bini Markham.

"Yeah, it's been done. There was a paper almost ten years ago on simulating high-acceleration aerosol dispersion patterns by, ah"—he paused with an embarrassed look—"by Bannerjee and Gold."

"I sent you an email days ago about that."

"I know, I just … well I've been focused on tracking Palestinians."

"Well, I think that with this connection we may have Gold and Bannerjee nailed. It's enough to go on, anyway. We still don't have anything direct to tie in Hargrove, but this Brit is beginning to smell like a crock of bad Stilton. Let's bring them in, lean on all three, and go through everything with a fine-toothed comb. And a Geiger counter."

She waited, but no one moved. She looked to Lev, who said, "Let's go, girls and boys." The room cleared.

Lev took his time gathering his papers. "It's not about you, Anat. It's me. I'm still here. In the way. They will … respect … orders. When I'm gone."

Anat was about to enter her own office just as Rahel came bouncing out of hers across the hall. "Do you think Lev is getting any better, Rahel?" she said, as she opened her door. "I am not sure being at the office and working so much is all that good for him. What do you think?"

Rahel pursed her lips for a moment. "I think you worry too much. Lev is a big boy. He can decide for himself. Besides, nobody ever tells Lev Novikov what to do, least of all a female.

Except for his mother, and I do believe she gave up on him when he was thirteen."

"I just, you know, worry."

"He means a lot to you, doesn't he?"

Anat was taken aback by the candor. First Shira Markham and now Rahel. Am I that transparent? she thought. "Of course, he does," she said. "He means a lot to all of us in the section. It's not like there's anything going on, if that's what you're implying."

"No, not what I mean. But surely you know that Lev is interested."

Anat touched her lower lip with the tip of a finger. Okay, she thought, we'll have it this way. "You really think so? I don't see it. Frankly, I think maybe you have more of a chance than me."

Rahel laughed. "Oh, sister, what you do not know."

Anat tried not to let her annoyance show. "Look, I've seen you coming on to him. And you two spend a lot more time together than he and I do. Did. Maybe it's a little different since I took over for him. But admit it. You have a bit of a thing for him, too."

"Like I said, what you do not know, Anat. Look, I have a partner already. Tzipi and I have been together for nearly five years. She's all I want. I'm not interested in Lev. I'm not even interested in boys."

Anat stammered, "But, but I've seen you flirting with him. I don't get it."

Rahel smiled and put her hand on Anat's shoulder. "Stroking the male ego. He likes it, likes to have his fantasies that I'm interested. Why should I spoil his fun? I like my job. I like Lev. I like working for him. I want to keep all that just as it is.

Lev is, well ... Lev is good with people as a phenomenon, but he's more than a little clueless when it comes to close relationships. I see no reason to spoil that, so I let him think I'm interested. But I'm in love with Tzipi and hope we can spend the rest of our lives together. So you see, Anat, the field is wide open, and you have a clear shot at the goal. I say go for it."

"But I never, I mean, you never ... I mean you have never said anything."

"First of all, it's not my place. He is my boss. And in case you might have forgotten, we are in the spy business here at Mossad. There are plenty of old timers who think gays and lesbians are security risks, and, although the official position has softened in recent years, the facts on the ground are little changed. I might not lose my job if certain people knew about Tzipi and me, but it would almost surely kill any chance for getting anywhere in the organization. Actually, given their methods, they probably do know, but as long as Tzipi and I keep a very low profile, I suspect they are prepared to tolerate us. It's a lot like that silly 'don't ask, don't tell' thing with the American military.

"Anyway, Lev is coming up on retirement. Do you think I want to become administrative assistant to whatever wet-behind-the-ears newbie nerd they stick in to replace him? No, I want to keep moving up. I know Lev thinks I'm content where I am, but that's just more of his interpersonal ignorance showing. I'm content working for Lev. For now. He's a great boss, as you know, but I'm not going to sit still forever."

"You know, Rahel, I might just be that newbie nerd that you could end up working for. If Lev retires while I'm still young enough to qualify as a newbie. Or still have my nerd credentials. Do you think you could work for me?"

"Of course. I'd be glad to help train you." She smiled warmly.

"Wow. I guess I've been put in my place."

"Not really. You just need to remember what you learned in field training. Keep your eyes open. Pay attention. Don't jump to conclusions." She started down the hall with her usual brisk bounce, then turned. "Frankly, if I was a switch-hitter rather than a confirmed leftie, I probably would take a crack at Lev. He is a good man. Even if he is just as clueless as any other male." She spun on her heel and took off.

Anat went into her office, closed the door behind her, and smiled broadly. Keep your eyes open. Pay attention. Don't jump to conclusions. Okay, she thought, good advice.

23

Chet Hargrove backed into the hallway and gently pulled the door of his hotel room closed, noting, in his thoughtful mood, what he had missed until now: the canted mezuzah on the doorjamb. Even in hotels, he thought, the trappings of the observant are everywhere. He stopped briefly at the elevator, then, changing his mind, headed for the stairwell and walked down the three flights to the ground floor. He strode across the brightly lit foyer with its outsized crystal chandelier and headed directly for the lobby bar. The bartender, a master of his trade, recognized him immediately and smiled. "The usual, Mr. Hargrove?" he asked as he continued to polish glasses.

"Not tonight, I think. Let me see your wine list." The

bartender handed him a double sided card from beneath the bar. Chet scanned it. "Do you have anything else, you know, something a little less ordinary?"

"I could get you the wine list from the restaurant. They have a bigger selection."

"Yes, please, do that."

Chet lit a cigarette while he waited for the bartender to return. Unlike his brother, who rarely was without a pipe or a cigar, Chet seldom smoked. But tonight was different. A cigarette seemed fitting.

The bartender returned with a thick, maroon plastic ring binder and passed it across the bar. Chet flipped through the pages, each neatly encased in its own plastic sleeve. He considered some of the Israeli wines before returning to the listing of French reds. He ordered a bottle of an excellent but terribly overpriced Bordeaux along with a cheese plate. He methodically finished off the cheeses and crackers and the entire bottle of wine by himself, then settled the tab in cash before marching out, grim faced, like a good soldier preparing for an assault on a distant beach. Outside, he asked the doorman to call a taxi and stood waiting, trying hard not to weave noticeably.

The taxi driver looked at his watch and sighed when Chet told him they were going to Jerusalem, but he sped off anyway. The next thing Chet was aware of was when the driver said, "Hey, we're here. Hey. Are you all right? We've arrived." Chet shook his head to clear it, thrust a handful of uncounted money at the driver as he clambered out of the car, then walked into the hospital.

Inside, he encountered some trouble at the nurses' station. He was, of course, quite drunk, although years of alcoholic practice helped him maintain a passable simulation of something resembling sobriety. It was a trick that did not always work, but this time, through careful concentration and resolute British calm, he was able to sustain the conversation with the charge nurse and ultimately to convince her that it was acceptable for him to be visiting in the middle of the night and to be left alone with his daughter.

He stood by the bed for several minutes, hands folded in front of him, listening to the rhythmic soughing of the ventilator and the steady beep of a monitor. He avoided looking at Clarissa's bandaged face and instead stared at her arm while he stroked her limp hand.

He spoke softly to her, his voice a sodden whisper. "I know I was not a good father. I know I was a damper on your every impulse from the time you were just a toddler to when you went to boarding school as a teen. I was never tolerant of exuberance or outbursts any more than was my father. Perhaps I wanted some of that energy of yours, somehow, I suppose, but I could never handle it. And I didn't expect to be raising you alone. I didn't expect your mother to be gone so much, to be so ... So, what? So successful? So unavailable? So uncaring?

"I cannot watch you die and I cannot watch you live, not this way," he said, in a voice that choked into a squeak at the end as he began to cry. He slipped off his shoes and arranged them neatly under the bed, then lowered the safety railing and climbed awkwardly up onto the high hospital bed. "Clarissa," he whispered as he curled up beside her. He reached into his pocket and withdrew the handful of pills. Enough, yes it will be enough, he thought, especially after the wine. He swallowed them without water, in a single gulp, just as he had been taught by his father. "Clarissa," he whispered again as he began to drift into a dizzy sleep. "Agneta," he said, as he slipped his arm over his daughter's body.

Anat waltzed into Lev's office with a stack of papers under her arm. "We got another body," she said dramatically.

"Huh?"

"Another suicide, only this one is the real thing, not an execution. They found the other Hargrove, the brother, curled up on the bed beside his daughter at *Sha'arei Tzedek*. Barbiturate overdose. So, we are not going to get anything of use from him nor can we expect a way finder to his brother.

"Oh, yes, a Doctor Harel there says they are now going to take the girl off the ventilator on the directions of her mother, who seems to have left the country shortly after signing the consent forms."

"Get someone up there," Lev said. "In case. Hargrove may show. Next of kin."

Daniel did not think they were yet hot on his trail, but he hated having to return to *Sha'arei Tzedek*. Still, someone had to identify his brother's body. What an idiot, he thought, what a meaningless way to die. The hospital morgue was cold and stark, much as expected, and the identification had been a mechanical formality that Daniel resented mostly because it took him away from more important matters and because it involved his despised brother. They had asked him what to do with the body, and he had said simply, "Burn it!" full knowing the Jewish attitude toward cremation. He apologized, making excuses about all the stress of the bad fortune befalling his family and promising to make arrangements for the body to be picked up. In truth, he had no idea what his brother's wishes were, but then he had little inclination to follow them even if known. As far as he was concerned, Izzy had led a pointless life and had punctuated it with a pointless death.

"Do you want to see your niece while you are here," the nurse at the desk asked him.

Daniel wanted to say no, but something impelled him to nod, dumbly. A volunteer escorted him to the floor and pointed toward the room. Daniel strode in without slowing and then stopped.

"I am sorry. I must have the wrong room."

The young woman kneeling by the bed turned his way. "Oh, you must be her uncle. She talked so much about you. She thought you were something amazing."

Daniel scowled. "She did? And you are?"

"I'm Mafalda José. Josie. I'm Lissie's friend."

"What? Who's friend?" Daniel asked in a voice tinged by growing confusion. Felicity Gold sometimes went by Lissie.

"Clarissa. We all called her Lissie. We go ... went to school together." She stood and held out her hand to Daniel, who had to reach down to take it. "I am so sorry for you. You must have been close," she said.

"We ... I ..." He shook his head as if to clear it. "She talked about me?"

"All the time. I think you were the father she wished she had. Although I didn't think her father was really all that bad. I do think he really loved her. That's why he couldn't bear to see her like this. Did you know they took her off the ventilator? She's still hanging on, though. A strong heart and a willful spirit."

"I don't know about her heart," Daniel said, recovering his composure, "but her spirit, if you wish to call it that, was reamed out of her by an Israeli bullet some days ago."

"I meant, well …" She sighed. "You don't believe, do you? You don't believe in God or heaven or anything. Like your Princes, who battle error and unreason and idolatry. I've read them all, the whole series. Lissie, too. For me, I think you were the one who first showed me the way."

"The way?"

"The way out of the confines of my Catholic convictions, a way to a moral life without scripture or fantasy. I do think your Princes are too strident, but then they are not battling actual believers or real religions; they are fighting imaginary foes, the Theochrons and the Ghosters and the Heironomy. So, I forgive you."

Daniel, completely taken aback, said nothing.

"I think it's time, though. She needs to go. As you do, as I do, as we all do, eventually."

"I am afraid I am not following you, young lady," he said, recovering some of his usual arrogance.

"Do it. Do it yourself, even, or find someone who can."

Daniel finally realized what she was talking about. Since his niece could breathe on her own, it had become more difficult to end it. He didn't know what the laws were in Israel. Perhaps one would have to arrange for medical transport to another, more tolerant jurisdiction. What a waste of money, he thought. He had no legal standing, of course, but perhaps he could help her mother finish what she had started. He shuddered at the thought of having to deal with Agneta. Still, it was a noble cause. But perhaps there was a simpler, a more direct way.

"I have found someone," he said, suddenly inspired. "You. You were her friend. You were far closer to her than was I. And now it is your responsibility. Find a way." He turned and left abruptly.

Mafalda José stared at the doorway. "'As it has been charged, so it will be discharged,'" she said aloud, quoting the Knights of Brilliandi as they had assembled in the courtyard of the Princes before riding off to do battle with the Ghoster invaders. "You are right," she said, turning from the closing door toward the bed, "a friend does have responsibilities."

She gently lifted her friend's head and slowly slid the pillow from beneath it.

Part Three

24

I thought you said no dress rehearsals. No face-to-face," Felicity said with undisguised impatience. "So why are we here, together, in the lab."

They were surrounded by an assortment of equipment that made complete sense only to Roger. On the door it said Meir E. Slansky Particulates Research Lab. Funded by a large and unexpected grant to the university and coordinated by an absent multinational consortium that remained absent and did little or nothing in the way of coordinating, the lab had been set up in the basement of a disused building near the edge of campus where it would not bother anyone. Hebrew University had been only too happy to accept the generous capital addition along with the yearly payments for operating expenses plus a

187

generous contribution to overhead. This was, after all, simply how the business of academia operated in the twenty-first century.

"This is not a dress rehearsal," Roger explained, "only a system check. We turn everything on, run through the pre-op checks, ping all the devices, and make sure it is all ready to go. You don't have to be here, but I thought you might want to watch as it all checked out."

He turned on his laptop and plugged the bulky transceiver into a USB port on the back. The disk churned, the screen turned blue and prompted him for his user name and password. He typed, then pressed his thumb to the fingerprint scanner in the corner of the machine. The screen went blank and stayed blank. Roger hit the Escape key, then the Enter key, then banged away repeatedly. "Weird," he said. "Some gremlin. I'll power down for a hard reboot and try again." A second try yielded the same results. Felicity and Daniel said nothing but exchanged nervous glances as Rajid went through the sequence a third time. "This is decidedly weird," he said before trying a "three-finger salute," the conventional cry for help of Windows users everywhere. He pressed the CTRL, ALT, and DELETE keys at the same time and was at last rewarded by the comforting sound of the disk churning away and his desktop filling in.

"Very odd, that, but now we seem to be ready to go." He opened a directory and scrolled down until he found the master control program and double-clicked. The screen repainted with an enormous smiley face above a Hebrew inscription. "What the fuck? What does that mean," he asked, pointing at the Hebrew words.

"It means we're fucked. It says *HaRuach Chai*, the living

spirit." She laughed. "You, oh Roger the Wonk, have a virus. You must have been visiting the seedier side of the Web in your spare time. Or gathering Hassidic propaganda."

"I swear, I tell you the comm center, FaceFolder, is the only place I have ever gone with this thing. That's it. I can't imagine how this happened."

He hit escape and the screen cleared, but whatever program he tried to launch he got the same leering yellow face. "I'll have to try and decontaminate this thing. That could take time." He started a scan with his anti-virus software only to have the intruding smiley face appear after a few seconds. "Shit, double shit!"

"Relax. Don't worry." Felicity put a hand on his arm. "We'll use mine. It has never been on Wi-Fi and has been used for one and only one purpose. No porn, no Twitter, no nothing." She pulled an identical laptop out of her briefcase and powered it up.

"You have to plug in the transceiver first," Roger said impatiently.

"Hold your horses, hotshot. I'll get there one step at a time." She finished booting up and opened a text editor. It flashed briefly on the screen, only to be replaced by the same stupid smiley face.

Daniel was laughing.

Felicity glared at him. "I fail to see how this can be funny. This is serious, you jerk. What the hell are we going to do now?"

"Use a real machine," he said, slipping his MacBook Pro out of its two-tone sueded leather sleeve. "I keep telling you guys to switch to a real computer, a reliable computer, one that doesn't wobble like a bent gyroscope whenever you install

updates, that doesn't get infected with viruses and Trojans."
He opened the screen with a flourish and was almost instantly
rewarded by a pleasant tone and the familiar desktop. "And
you don't have to wait ten minutes while Windows boots up.
Instant gratification." He stroked the edges of the screen sen-
suously and pretended to flick a bit of dust from one of the
keys. "Beautiful." He gloated. "And it works!" He clicked on
an icon in the Dock, which popped up and grew like a genie
out of a bottle. "So lovely." He gestured at the screen, which
suddenly was filled with a big yellow grin above a Hebrew cap-
tion.

Roger and Felicity were both practically doubled over with
laughter.

"What the …? This is utterly impossible. Macs simply
cannot get viruses. Hang on just a minute. Did you two do
this? Is this some kind of puerile prank? Because, if it is, it is
not funny. This could completely cripple the Initiative."

Roger was shaking his head, trying to get his snickering
under control. "No, I didn't do it, and I don't think Lissie
would know how anymore. No, this is some serious shit."

"But Macs can't get viruses," Daniel protested again, as he
shook his head in disbelief.

"Another urban legend. Simply not true. In fact, Macs are
becoming more and more vulnerable, in part because so few
Macs are running anti-virus protection and in part because the
hackers are looking for new intellectual challenges, better ways
to show off how clever they are. And this 'living spirit' is one
damned clever virus, what they call a polymorphic vector. It
appears that it can change form to infect different operating
systems. No, it's no joke. We've been had! Big time. The whole
Initiative might have to be scrubbed, all because of some god-

damned virus."

"Hang on there," said Daniel. "All we need is another computer, a clean one. All the software is sitting on the server. We go to the website, download all the programs and scripts, and we're up and running again."

Roger shook his head. "Not likely, Daniel. Tell me, what is the one thing these three infected machines have in common? If you take us at our word—and believe me, I for one am telling the truth—the only site we have visited is our own. Somebody has snuck in the back door, some hackers, some kids, maybe, and messed with our site. It's contaminated. We go there and odds are we infect any new machine we use. No, we can't go that route."

"We have to do something. We're dead without that software. This can't be pulled off completely manually. You know that. We have to get fresh copies of the software. It has to be the current versions that have been debugged with the simulators."

"Okay, so where is our server."

"The Cayman Islands. Angola. Who knows? It's all virtual. We pay by the month and by the gigabyte and they host it. For all I know, it moves every few weeks. Or maybe it's in the goddamned 'cloud' as you techies call it."

Felicity held up a finger. "But. There's a mirror, a backup copy. It's right here in the building."

"Won't that be infected, too?"

"Maybe not. When did you last use your laptop? Yesterday? Yesterday morning? Okay. Things worked then, so we may be good. The backup is on a weekly cycle. Although it depends on when the virus was planted and whether there was a delay built in, but the mirror copy could be good. As long as we isolate it before," she looked at her watch, "before 18:00 today. So, I'll borrow a clean laptop from a colleague in the mobile computing lab and try sucking the software directly off the mirror server. Roger, you get to a public terminal and see if you can post a message warning off the rest of our network. Then let's wipe and rebuild your and my systems and try again."

"What do I do?" asked Daniel.

"Find a rubbish bin and scrap that elegantly styled designer doorstop of yours," Roger said, pointing to the Mac-Book.

"Aren't we going to rebuild it, too?"

"Can't. Don't know how," Roger told him. "You'll have to go to the Genius Bar for that. The nearest Apple store is in Tel Aviv, it opened late 2008. You can call and make an appointment. They can probably fit you in within a few days, a week or two at the most." He grinned at Daniel, who sputtered and left the room.

Felicity gave Roger a look. "Really? You don't know how to rebuild a MacBook? I thought you could do anything. Nuclear physics, explosives, aerodynamics, automation, operating systems. The mind boggles."

"I could do it. But I won't. I hate those ... those things. Eye candy. Give me an ugly, versatile Wintel machine any day. We better get cracking, though; we have a lot to do before we're ready to retry the systems check."

Just then Felicity's cell beeped for an incoming message. She opened it and gasped. "My secretary. Says I am wanted 'for questioning.' They've found us. I knew it. I knew this would happen. We could never pull it off."

"Don't be a weak sister, Lissie. Let's get those files off the mirror, grab Daniel, and shift venues. We don't need the lab anymore. We are good to go already. We go to ground, just as planned."

Karl paced back and forth, gingerly navigating the littered floor of Bini's once-again appropriately messy bedroom, avoiding discarded socks and stepping around schoolbooks. Something crunched underfoot, and he bent down to pick up a broken printed circuit board with the legend "Slade Controls" just visible on its margin. He turned it over several times in his hand before setting it on the dresser.

"Tell me what you did, exactly," he said.

"We planted a virus, a Trojan on their site, a selective sleeper that infects everyone who ever visits the site but only becomes active for anyone who posts or reads hidden messages."

"Jeezus. Do you have any idea what you've done? You not only may have tipped them off or scared them off, you may have messed up the computers at the Institute. Did you think of that? Lev is reading those messages, too."

"Geez, we didn't think of that. We were just trying to help, you know, to do something."

"Well, don't help. Don't do something. You can look but don't touch. I do not want you trying anything again without first checking with me and with your Uncle Lev. Do you hear? And I thought you had been told to go dark, stay clear."

"But Abba Karl, we ..."

"No buts. Nothing, nada, without checking with us first. Shit, I better get on the phone to Lev right away. Meanwhile, is there anything you can do to disinfect the site, I mean stop the virus?"

"Yeah, duh. We're not script-babies. We hand coded the whole thing ourselves. Damned clever, too, like polymorphic so it can infect different kinds of machines. See it has this script that detects the operating system before downloading the right version and ..."

"I don't care. I don't want to hear about how smart it is. I am more concerned about how not-smart you and your friends are. So kill it, quick. Wipe it out. Hit the undo button with great vigor. Okay?" He pulled his cellphone from his pocket as he stomped out of the room.

When Lev finally answered, his speech was thick and punctuated by odd pauses. "Yes? Whassup?" he said. Karl told him. "Oh. That. We know. Soft ... software spotted it. Days ago. Figured it out fast. No problem. Won't hurt us. Didn't know who. Bini and kids. Shoulda guessed. Hope gang doesn't bolt before ... we close in." He hung up without saying goodbye. Poor guy, thought Karl.

25

Pyotr stepped into the office and interrupted Lev's conversation with Anat. "You know that the girl died," he said. "The student who was shot. Actually she was murdered, technically speaking. Seems that someone put a pillow over her head sometime after the hospital took her off the ventilator. They are looking for her American classmate who was one of the last two people to see her. Guess who the other one was. Our very own Clarkson Daniel Hargrove. Want to take odds on which one of them they find first?"

Anat smiled grimly. "No thanks. With Clarkson pulling a disappearing act, it seems that Hargroves are vanishing one by one before our very eyes. Our team must have missed him by mere minutes at the hospital." She turned back to Lev. "Are you coming for the morning briefing? I'm afraid it's pretty much all gloom and doom all the way from the headlines to the comic pages."

Lev smiled up at her. "Why not," he said, reaching for her outstretched hand.

As if not wanting to waste even seconds, Anat started talking as soon as she entered the room. "We have now lost track of Hargrove, Bannerjee, *and* Gold, which would be completely bad news except that it pretty much clinches some kind of a tie-in among the three of them. We are guessing that Bannerjee is the one identified as the Wonk in the decoded signed postings, and that Gold is the Wizard, making Hargrove the Sage. We are analyzing the backlog of decoded messages with that in mind to see if there is anything else we can tease out that might give us a clue as to where they are or precisely what they are up to. That's where we are. Anyone got anything?" Anat looked around the table but got nothing but headshakes.

"Such enthusiasm! Look, people, we are standing on the edge of a precipice here, and it's pitch dark, and we do not know what is waiting for us below. We need intelligence, rumors, speculations, I don't care what, but give me something, damn it."

Lev nodded approvingly beside her. "At this rate," he said, "Karl will beat us to the ... to them. Who are the pros now?" His cellphone rang, he looked at the caller ID, and he handed the phone to Anat without answering it.

Anat and Pyotr stood with Rafi Yadin outside the Slansky Lab. Rafi pulled a little box from his bag, held it in front of the electronic lock, and pressed a button. A powerful electromagnetic pulse overloaded whatever was inside, and the door lock released with a loud thunk. Anat followed Rafi, and Pyotr stopped just inside the door. "I think we found the plant," he said, looking down at his Geiger counter. He scanned the room, taking in the mix of laboratory gear and industrial process equipment. Rafi started wandering around the facility, looking closely at several of the various boxes and instruments.

"Let's do a once over," Pyotr said, "then get a team up here to check for prints. And some hazmat boys to see what they can make of what's been in some of these centrifuges and mixers."

Anat turned to leave. "I'll go back to the admin people to see what if anything they have in their records about the Lab and what has been going on here. I'm not counting on much, but you never know, something might be useful."

As Rafi continued to peer and poke around, Pyotr kneeled down to look at something on the floor. "Cigar ash. We can make a guess about whose." As he pushed himself back up, his Geiger counter passed by the ash, and the indicator bar jumped on the display. "As they say, people who play with fire. I wonder if he knows?"

His parents were out for a stroll when Bini woke up his computer again. He knew he probably should not be on the computer at all, certainly not doing what he was about to attempt. Uncle Lev, the Anat woman, and Abba Karl had all told him to stop messing around. No, they had said for his group to cease its activities, to go dark. They had done that. They had shut down their chat room and stopped emailing, right in the middle of their biggest project. And he had dutifully sent the suicide code to their clever virus to shut itself down and pass the message on down the line, just as he had been told. Still, there was one more thing, one more irresistible something to do. It was not like they were planting another virus. He accessed the FaceFolder site through his backdoor key, got a prompt, and worked his way down through the directory structure. There it was, the file he was looking for. He noted the file size, date and time stamp, then modified his own file to match. He then started a file transfer from his system to the distant server. There. Done. He closed the connection, and started to shut down his computer. Wait, I should get the latest copies of those maps. He switched to the biblical archeology site and started downloading files. Got to get some sleep and get an early start, too, he thought, as he lay down.

Karl sipped the last dregs from his coffee mug and rubbed his eyes. Time to pack it in, he thought. Something was nagging at him, but it eluded him, lurking just below conscious thought. He reluctantly closed his laptop, slipped it into his backpack, picked up his mug, rinsed it in the sink, then carefully dried it.

On his way to the bedroom, he looked in on Bini, who was sleeping on a diagonal across the bed with one arm dangling over the side. He had fallen asleep without even turning off his computer. Karl squeezed past the end of the bed to shut down the laptop. He closed the "Download complete" message stuck on the screen, then put the laptop to sleep. He smiled as he drew a coverlet over the sleeping form on the bed. At least you're out of this damned business about the Dome, he thought. Now if I can just get Shira to leave well enough alone.

As he left the room, he brushed past the dresser, knocking

something to the floor. It was the broken circuit board, which he retrieved and replaced atop the dresser. That's my Bini, he thought, always collecting the damnedest things. As he reached to turn off the light, the printing along the edge caught his eye: Slade Controls. Suddenly he remembered how Bini had come by the fragment, and finally realized where it was that he had first seen Clarkson Hargrove. This is significant, he thought. I should pass this on to Lev and Anat. He looked at his watch. Very late. He could email, but it would not likely be seen until morning anyway. I'll call in the morning. He turned off the light and headed for bed.

26

nat was at her desk before six in the morning. She was not surprised when Lev walked by and dropped a traffic summary on her desk. He stood and waited while she quickly skimmed the near-empty page. She looked up at him with a puzzled expression.

"Call Karl," he said.

She nodded and punched Karl's shortcut code. He answered on the first ring.

"It's Anat. Sorry to bother you at this hour, but something is definitely going on. After days of multiple postings, the FaceFolder site went silent, then last night, just past midnight, we found one more message. The plaintext is just one word, but it doesn't make sense. At first we thought it might be Arabic, but no. A name? We haven't a clue."

"What is it? What was the message?"

"Jarhinah," she said, reading from the traffic summary, then spelling it out.

"Sounds like maybe a literary reference," he said. "I think I recognize it. Let me check on a hunch. Hold on a moment." He pulled out his laptop, booted up, and went immediately to Amazon.co.uk. He typed "Clarkson Hargrove" in the search box and quickly got back a page full of book blurbs. The second one down, with only a placeholder graphic instead of a thumbnail cover image next to it, caught Karl's eye."

"It's today," he said.

"What? How do you know?"

"Hargrove once told me about struggling with his publisher over the closing chapters of his next book. He said that he and only he would determine how and when the world ended. According to no less an authority than Amazon.co.uk, the final volume of, quote, the award-winning epic fantasy saga of the Princes of Pelucida, unquote, is titled '*Vengeance at Jarhinah*.' I remember now. In the series, Jarhinah is the City of Peace. Get it? *Yerushalayim*. City of Peace."

"At least that's one possible meaning, Karl, according to popular mythology, which would certainly make Jerusalem a leading contender as the most ironically misnamed city in the world. Okay, etymology aside, if you're right, we have to move fast. Let me assemble the team and get some things started, then I'll call you back. Can you get to a phone where you can stay on the line with us, like, maybe all day?"

"When you're ready, Skype me. That will be easier on my end." He hung up.

She took a deep breath and turned to Lev. Oddly, he was

smiling at her, an affectionate smile.

"Okay. Okay," she said, as much to herself as to Lev. "IDF, military intelligence, police, we'll need a SWAT team standing by, bomb squad, decontamination. Who did I forget?"

"*Hel HaAvir*," he said, referring to the Israeli air corps. "Yadin," he added.

She scowled. "Right, Shin Bet. But you know they'll grab the reins, Yadin or somebody else. No matter who is in, we are going to be on the outside looking in on this, and it's our baby. It's been our case from the start."

"Who cares. Stay in the loop. Remember what matters."

"Okay, let's start by getting the entire area evacuated and cordoned off. Should not be too hard at this hour, but we have to move fast."

"No," he said. "Start with the boss. Channels. He'll call Bibi," he said, referring to the prime minister.

"Right. Sorry." She reached for her secure phone.

By the time Anat arrived at the situation room, nearly all of Lev's team and most of the other section leads were already gathered, and the room rustled with hurried, parallel conversations. They were surrounded by screens displaying feeds from other agencies as well as the TV stations. A public announcement had already been made in Jerusalem and, no surprise, news coverage was beginning. Television crews were already amassing just outside the IDF lines and badgering the spokespersons for every agency they could track down.

The Palestinians had hit the roof about clearing the Temple Mount and cordoning it off, until Yadin had overstepped his authority and told them what was really going on. Even so, they insisted on joining in supervising the evacuation and in policing the lines.

Lev tapped his pen on the table until the room quieted, then said, "Anat. Dorfman. Acting Chief of ..." He paused, looked down at the table in embarrassment and frustration at not finding the word, then said, "of us."

Anat stood as he sat down. "Lev's modest. He's still really in charge, but we split responsibilities. He does the thinking and I do the talking." There was a brief, quiet ripple of nervous laughter. "So, here's what we have and what we're looking at, for those of you who are not completely up on Operation Chit-chat." She shifted gears and started firing off details like a Gatling gun, trying as quickly as possible to bring everyone up to speed on the operation.

"So," she said, "to wrap up, we still are only making a best guess about where to look, and we have no idea what to look for, but we're pretty sure it's coming. Today. The whole area of the Temple Mount is being cleared and cordoned off as we speak."

"All this on the hunch of your asset? Some techie blogger?" It was Benji ben Aviv, youngest of the section chiefs and generally regarded as a pain in the *tukas*.

Lev stood up and started to speak, but Anat put her hand on his arm. "As I told everyone, we split the responsibilities, so I'll explain." He sat down again.

"Karl Lustig is a journalist and a consultant. He has had connections with the Institute for many years. Almost single-handed, he tracked down the missing MIT material for us and, incidentally, once saved the life of our esteemed Chief of Technical Services." She nodded toward Lev. "On this particular operation, we would still be nowhere without his contribution.

In fact, I'm patching him in to our meeting because we need him. Are you there, Karl? Can you hear us?"

"Yeah, fine. Go ahead."

Dov Begin, in charge of internal security, looked up from his laptop and raised a finger. "Says here he's American. We can't have this. It's a complete breach of security. And I still say we're stupid to do something like this on a hunch from an American ex-pat who earns a few shekels by writing blogs about Israeli technology. I say ..."

He was interrupted by Shimon Weiszkopf, who entered the room puffing and panting. "We got another bot denial-of-service attack. The barbarians hordes are pounding at our gates again."

"That's it!" Lev said, slapping the table with an open hand. "Proves it."

Anat jumped in. "This is no coincidence. They want to overwhelm us, cut us off, while they pull off the job. The last attack was only a test, just as Lev suggested at the time."

Shimon grinned. "Won't work. I made some changes after the last attack. We now have virtual tunnels that let us get through and around the DOS attack. The public still won't be able to access our website, but all our comms are still good, even VOIP, and we still have full Internet access." His grin broadened. "They should never have warned us."

Lev kept nodding. "Good. Good work, Shimon, good."

Shimon was grinning. He was suddenly hero of the day. As he found a place at the big conference table he wore the slightly smug expression of the schoolyard runt who had finally redeemed himself.

The buzz around the table was interrupted by the Director General entering the room, which hushed as he made his way to his seat at the head of the table.

"I've briefed the Prime Minister and touched base with all the other agencies involved. There has been a pretty intense exchange over who is in charge. The bad news is that it will not be us. The PM says it has to be someone on the ground, and we are not there. We're here, in a bunker in Tel Aviv. On the other hand, it is unclear whether this is a domestic or international threat, a civil or a military matter. The possibilities and the posturing could go on and on. The good news is the PM shut everyone up and simply put Shin Bet in charge as far as intelligence is concerned, and they in turn made our colleague Rafi Yadin field operations lead. He has promised to coordinate closely with us, particularly with Lev's team, which has done so much of the legwork. Or should I say, finger work?" He looked around, expecting a chuckle.

Lev broke the silence. "Good one," he said, miming typing at a keyboard, which got a laugh.

"Can I interrupt?" Karl's voice boomed out from an overhead speaker.

"Sure, Karl, any time," said Anat.

"I think I may have a guess about the delivery method they're using. Ever since I first met Hargrove at the conference in Haifa, I have been bothered by a nagging feeling that I had seen him before, and I don't mean his photo, which is plastered on book jackets and posters and flashed on TV everywhere. No, I was sure I had actually seen him in person, but I just couldn't remember where or when. So, anyway, I finally put it together last night when I came across this piece of a circuit board that my son had once salvaged from the beach at Ga'ash. He had retrieved it from a wrecked glider that had crashed on the beach, a radio-control rig, semi-autonomous as I surmised, that appeared to be getting its instructions from a computer being used by a tall gentleman scrunched into a small Fiat. When the aircraft crashed, the man did the strangest thing; he just drove off. He didn't seem to care what happened to the plane and made no attempt to salvage anything from the wreck. I remembered his face, though, and I now realize it was Clarkson Hargrove, though I didn't make the connection at the time. Does the name Slade Controls mean anything to anyone there?"

Anat looked around the situation room. Pyotr spoke up. "It's here on the inventory of goods found in the apartment of that murdered supplier," he said, pointing at his laptop screen. "There was a whole box of things from Slade Controls."

There was silence in the room.

"It's an aerial attack, I'm almost certain," Karl interjected, "because I also tracked down an interview on YouTube from several years ago in which Hargrove said that his hobby, his passionate hobby, was flying radio-controlled planes."

"You think he's using a glider?" someone asked. "That doesn't make sense. A glider big enough to carry the bomb we think they need would be, would be enormous. And how would he launch it?"

"Not a glider, necessarily, but something like it, with oversized wings for extra lift. And maybe not really radio-controlled. My son found this code on their site that is some kind of robot control program, so maybe a UAV, an unmanned aerial vehicle: a drone, an autonomous or semi-autonomous drone. Something that could carry a lot of weight. My guess is that it would be something fairly slow, with a limited range. If it were coming from too far away it would have to be a full-size plane and would also be too vulnerable, giving too much advance warning. I suspect it's right in your backyard, only you don't know it. Somewhere in the West Bank, maybe."

"We are already watching the skies pretty closely. I don't think anything in the air could take us by surprise."

"But this thing would not fly very high. Climbing to altitude costs extra fuel. This thing could easily come in under the radar. Visual contact might be your first warning."

Anat turned to the Director. "We need chopper surveillance. And we should task a satellite for real-time imaging. We have got to find that thing. Before it finds the Dome."

"Do you have any idea what tasking a satellite for real-time views is going to cost? And I'm not even sure there's one in position or even close."

"We have one," said Rina, one of the technicians from Weiszkopf's team, "that can give us eyes-on in …" She typed a few strokes. "A little over four minutes?"

Anat spoke next. "Thanks, Rina." She turned to face the Director, "Look, surely we can resolve the budget issues later. If there is still a budget or an agency to resolve anything. Right now we need eyes."

The Director nodded. "All right, all right. We'll get the satellite. I'll okay it. As soon as you have an image, put it up on that screen."

"I have a downlink now, and an uplink for control," Rina reported.

"You what? How did you do that?"

"I put in the request as soon as our asset told us what we were looking for. Made sense." She smiled and Anat gave her an approving nod, then turned back to the group.

"So, what are we looking for? Exactly? Any ideas Karl?" Silence. "Karl, are you there?"

"Er, yeah, I was just in the other room, looking for my son. What was the question?"

"What are we looking for? We have aerial recon from Blackhawks over Jerusalem and satellite real-time imaging in another minute or so. There, it looks like it's about to come online. What would this thing look like?"

"If it's out in the open, look for a big cross, with the wings maybe longer than the body. I have no idea about dimensions or whether it would even show on a satellite image. That's why I wanted my son. He's good at estimating things, and he might be able to say how big the glider was that we saw. He's off somewhere, though. But, if it's covered up or camouflaged, it could look like anything. Or nothing."

"What do we do if we do spot it?" she asked looking around the table.

"I know what we must not do," Pyotr said. "We must not blow it up. If we have to sit on it to keep it from taking off, then we sit, but no grenades, rockets, tank shells, or anything that could trigger it."

"I've got it, I think," Dov interrupted, pointing at the projection of the satellite view. "There. See that, that cross. Could that be our plane?"

"Looks like it could be. That's in an area under the PA. Rafi, you there."

"I'm here."

"You need to get some men in there. Now. Here are the coordinates." She turned to Rina at the uplink controls, who positioned a cursor and read off the coordinates from bottom of the screen. "Got that?"

"Yeah."

"Then get some men over there. Make sure nobody uses

any firearms or does anything that might make it blow."

"What are we supposed to do, then? Sit on it?"

"I don't know. Be creative. Tie it down. Break off its wings. Anything, but just don't let it take off."

"I need authorization. I have to clear it with the PA. I need the authority."

"The PM is on the line. He says he gave you virtual carte blanche. This is a national emergency. What more do you need? Just do it. We'll ask forgiveness from the Authority later."

"It's too late. We'll never get there in time."

"How the fuck do you know how much time we have. We have to try."

"It may not even be a plane. This could be a wild goose chase. It could be a decoy. We don't know."

"Then get over there and find out, goddamnit."

"Sir," it was a techie with a headset across the room. "We have eyes on the bird. A spotter in the area with a high-powered telescope confirms it's a plane."

"Did you hear that Rafi? Rafi?" There was no sound from the speakers. "Somebody, give me a phone. Mine won't work down here. Anyone, anyone got any bars?"

Rahel pulled a pink RAZR from her purse, checked it, and handed it to Anat. "What are you going to do?"

"Call him on his personal cellphone and hope he answers."

"Rafi, what are you doing?" she asked in a voice low enough to make it hard for others to hear.

"I don't think we can stop it, and I don't think we should even if we can."

"Are you serious?"

"This would put an end to all the fighting."

"Don't be crazy. The fighting won't stop, they'll just be fighting over fuckin' radioactive rubble. Nuking the Dome is not going to solve anything. They'll all just be killing each other over something new."

"I can't. I think this group has the right idea. I think it's time we got rid of it all."

"Look, if this turns into orders from the PM or your superiors, it could be charges of treason. Rafi?"

"Sir," the comms operator said to the Director, "the IDF is going in."

"Shit, do they know what they're up against?"

"It's a special forces team; they've been briefed."

The Director, talking with someone on a private line, held up his hand for attention. "A spotter on a tower just reported he saw something like a jet taking off from an olive grove, then this big-winged plane passed right overhead and dropped what looked like a couple of bombs except they didn't explode. Air corps is getting their choppers over for a closer look at ..." he read off map coordinates. At the satellite uplink console, Rina brought the area into view, but nothing was evident. She started to zoom in.

"I knew it," said Pyotr. "Rocket-assisted take-off. That's what the solid rockets were for on the list we got from the Egyptian's apartment. I wondered just how they would get a lumbering bird like that airborne."

"One of our Blackhawks has eyes-on." The Director called out. "A bogie. It's six minutes out at present speed and bearing, they say. They're asking their command for permission to shoot it down."

"Six minutes. Fuck!" somebody snapped.

"No!" shouted Lev. "Don't let them. No. It's ... uh ..."

Anat finished for him: "It's radioactive. It's a dirty bomb. They shoot it down and there's radioactive debris all over some part of Jerusalem."

"Well, it's either that or the Dome of the Rock, isn't it."

"No choice is also a choice," she said, turning to the Director. "Some residential neighborhood gets taken out or some empty monument. What would you pick?"

"But, we can't just do nothing," he answered.

"That's exactly what we must do at this point. You have to put it to the PM exactly that way. We can't shoot that thing down over a civilian area. We can't."

"I agree." It was Rafi Yadin's voice over the loudspeaker again. "I've asked the military to back off with their helicopters. It's a tough call, all right, but, well, maybe it could be for the best. I mean, the Dome, Al Aqsa, the Mosque?"

"And *HaKotel*. We lose the Wailing Wall."

"But maybe this is God's will?"

"I don't presume to know God's will, but this is clearly Clarkson Hargrove's will, just what he wanted, though I still can't fathom why."

The techie in the corner called out again. "Yadin's team has picked up a strong UHF signal, an intermittent data stream, from somewhere in East Jerusalem. They think it might be radio-control instructions."

"For God's sake, tell them to jam it if they can."

"They already are, but first they wanted to triangulate. They have a fix and are sending in a squad now."

"Can we get video from the Blackhawks? And can we zoom in on the Dome from the satellite shot?"

A screen on the left suddenly brightened with a jittery shot from one of the helicopters. The view in the other screen gradually grew larger. It reminded Lev of the Google Maps view he had first seen a week earlier.

"Good God that thing is big" Pyotr said, pointing at the image of the drone from the helicopter. "And will you look at the size of that nacelle hanging from under it. If my theory about a fuel-air detonation is right, we are going to see one hell of a fireball when that goes off. It will probably flatten the dome as well as disperse radioactive debris over the entire area. I wish we knew exactly how much was in there. We could run some simulations and plot the contamination area."

Anat shook her head. "We won't need any damned simulations. In a little less than two minutes we'll have the real thing and will know exactly how far it spreads. At least there's not much of a wind today. The stuff will pretty much settle out right where it is."

"Maybe we're okay," said Weiszkopf, hopefully. "I mean, we blocked the radio-control signal, didn't we?"

"I don't think it needs radio-control," Anat explained. "I think that's optional. It's a robot, semi-autonomous, runs on preprogrammed instructions." She bit her lip and said no more.

The room was silent as everyone watched the monitors. Anat leaned over to whisper a question to the Director.

"Yes, the decontamination teams are in place," he said quietly. "But they have to stay well back, and they have to wait for all clear from the fire brigade and the IDF. We've done all we could. Now we just wait."

Suddenly there was a grunt and a gasp from around the room. The drone could be seen just at the edge of the live satellite view, making a beeline for the center of the Dome. Nobody moved as it edged closer and closer.

"What's happening?" asked Karl.

"It's ..." Anat flinched involuntarily just as the drone reached the Dome. Someone cried out, then there was pandemonium in the room.

The Dome was still there. In the satellite view, the drone could be seen continuing in a straight line, heading toward Tel Aviv. A cheer went up around the conference table and could be heard over the audio as well.

"What happened? What happened?" It was Karl.

"We don't know, except that the bomb didn't go off over the Dome. It seems to be heading now toward us. Maybe we've been tricked, and it's Tel Aviv that's the target. Maybe we should shoot it down after all, try to pick a spot where the damage will be less than if it explodes over the Tel Aviv business district."

"Hold on a second," Karl said. "I was just scrolling the email on my son's machine, and there's a message here from one of his cronies in the amateur espionage network. It says ... Shit, those little creeps. They didn't stop when they were told. Surprise, surprise. If I understand what it says here, they hacked the flight-control code and disabled the drone. They put a no-op in an inner loop to prevent it from detonating at the computed target." He laughed. "I am sorry if this is getting way too technical. Basically, what they did seems to have worked, though."

"But can we trust what the email says? Can these kids really turn it into a complete dud?"

"We'll know in another few minutes."

They watched in silence as the satellite view showed the drone passing over Tel Aviv before heading out over the water, then disappearing from view.

"Blackhawk leader reports splashdown and no explosion. A recovery team is already on the way to try and retrieve it."

Lev expected the room to explode again, but aside from a few quick prayers, the room was quiet until Karl's voice interrupted. "Well?"

"Those kids are some hackers, Karl. It worked. The thing just died and fell into the water offshore. We think it's intact. No contamination. A recovery team is already on their way to the splashdown location."

"We were lucky," the Director pronounced solemnly. "We just dodged a bullet to the *Kipah*. Or *Kipat*." Groans and coughs spread through the room before it broke out in a burst of laughter. The Director looked quite pleased with himself.

27

People in the room began almost immediately to gather papers and equipment. Rina, at the satellite console, was about to relinquish control when the comms operator called out, "Wait! *Hel HaAvir* has another spotting. Looks like a small jet taking off from the West Bank adjacent to a lemon grove just a few miles from where the first drone launched. Yup, they have eyes-on. It's another one."

"What the hell? Another one? They can't have another one."

"Well apparently they don't know the meaning of 'can't,' because the chopper pilot says it looks like a twin of the other drone."

"Shit. How many do they have?"

"At least two."

Another voice cut in, with a lot of background noise. "This is Wing Commander, we … shit, the thing is dropping bombs. Do we shoot it down?"

"No! Don't shoot it down. Those are just the rocket-assist pods. Whatever you do, for God's sake, don't shoot it down."

Lev reached up toward Anat and signaled to her for a private chat. "Do we know if kids … programmed…all of them?" he said.

"No. Maybe only the one."

"Then listen," he said. He forced out the words one and two at a time until Anat nodded. She exhaled sharply and called out. "Tell the Wing Command we have an idea. So, can anyone here come up with an estimate of how fast that thing is going?"

"From the satellite image, it's making maybe 160 knots, there abouts," Rina answered. "Why?"

"Anyone know what our Blackhawks can do?"

Dov jumped in. "Top speed for those Blackhawks is 159 knots, according to this table. It could be close. The never-exceed speed is 193."

The pilot listened to the female voice in his headphones and said, "Go ahead. I'm listening."

"The plan is dirt simple," the voice said. "Get above the thing, sit on it, and push it to the ground, hopefully in some convenient place."

The pilot turned to his first officer. "Do you think we can do it?"

"It's worth a try."

"Then get back to the payload bay, clip into a harness,

plug in, and give me blow-by-blow on exactly where we are. Once we are over it, I can't trust the nose camera and I'll be blind. I want to catch that bastard right between our skids."

"What if we can't keep it down?"

"Once it's on the ground, it's going nowhere. It can't take off again. No rocket-assist. Get back there and give me eyes-on."

Moments later, the first officer started calling out continuous updates as the pilot raced after the drone and jockeyed for position. Suddenly the first officer shouted, "Right on! We're right above it."

"Okay, you bastard, elevator going down." The helicopter dropped sharply and slammed into the drone. As the pilot angled the Blackhawk and struggled to keep the drone cradled, its programs tried to compensate. The helicopter bucked and resisted the pilot's maneuvers, but he found that by flying at a slight angle to one side, he could keep the drone pushing itself against the skids and the underbody of the aircraft. He kept dropping, slowly, looking for a possible place for a forced landing. He spotted a small plaza almost in their flight path. He'd managed to slow considerably, but it would still be an iffy descent. There were several dozen pedestrians in the plaza, but there was little the pilot could do. He had his hands full keeping the drone beneath him and managing the approach. Suddenly he heard automatic weapons fire. The crowd below looked up and then started scattering in all directions.

"What happened?" the pilot asked.

"Our gunner just fired into the air. He thought you might prefer a clear landing pad."

"Thanks," the pilot said. At the last moment, he spun the helicopter around as it landed, sending it into a backwards, tipped-up slide across the plaza. He almost canceled the forward momentum before his tail rotor struck the wall of a building bordering the plaza. He killed the engines, settling the helicopter atop the drone, its weight breaking the wings and pinning them to the ground. The drone's prop kept spinning, futilely struggling to tug it free.

The pilot leaped out with his pistol drawn and emptied the clip at the blades of the propeller, which shattered, sending fragments flying. The engine of the drone whined as it spun out of control. Smoke began to stream from the front of the craft. His first officer rounded the corner from the other side, fire extinguisher in his hand. He hesitated and looked at the pilot, who shouted, "Do it!" The extinguisher hissed, and when it stopped, the plaza was quiet.

No one cheered this time in the situation room. They had been tricked into celebrating once; they wouldn't fall for it again.

Anat looked to the Director, who waved for her to proceed. "We are still on high alert, people. We don't know how many drones they have."

"Yes we do." It was Karl's voice over the loudspeaker.

"We do? How many?"

"Three."

"How can you know that? Or do you have intelligence we don't have."

"No, you have it, too. The Gold Standard. Triple redundancy. Get it? They have one shot. They do everything in triplicate. Dr. Gold would not have it any other way."

"Okay, we keep the choppers airborne, and we keep up satellite surveillance. Can we also program to watch for a burn from the rocket-assist? Good. And if nobody has done it yet, we should ground all flights."

"It's been done, long ago," someone in the back called out.

"Good. We know how to deal with it when it takes off. We just have to watch and wait until they make their last move."

It was a little over a half hour before Rafi called again. "We got to the site of the radio signal, but it was just a relay on top of an apartment building. It was already taken down by the time the second bird went up, so there was either another relay or they only needed it to start some kind of countdown."

"I'd bet there was another relay," Anat said, "and a third." She told him about the Gold Standard and about their theory regarding the group's strategy. "I don't suppose anyone has found any sign of Hargrove or the rest of the troika. So, we keep watching and waiting."

They watched and waited. The morning passed without incident, other than a brouhaha with a television news team that managed to breach the cordon around the Temple Mount area. Karl finally went offline after announcing he needed to check on something. People were beginning to talk about standing down when Rahel's pink phone rang again.

Anat discreetly picked it up.

"It's Rafi here. Look, I have something that I think maybe you and Lev should hear about first, before it gets into the regular channels. The police got a call awhile back from some missionary character or something, a Harold Timothy. Seems he has been doing archeological research underneath the Old City. Uses these little robots with cameras. Anyway, he was doing more research today, which he probably shouldn't have been doing, when one of his remote cameras spotted somebody. It was just a glimpse of someone scurrying past, but they capture everything on disk. So, anyway, he didn't bring this to anyone's attention right away because by then he had heard about the alert and was afraid of getting into trouble. Eventually, though, he called the police. Took him nearly an hour to get through to someone who understood what he was talking about and who passed him onto us. We had been checking into his group but not really watching too closely.

"Anyway, here's the deal. The figure in the shot is a boy. Can't see his face, but he's wearing a Boston Red Sox cap. According to this guy's map, the location would put him somewhere under *Har HaBayit*. The kicker is that their robot ended up just sitting there all day. I go to meet this Dr. Timothy at his van parked not far from *Har HaBayit*. Ten minutes ago somebody walks right up to the robot, bends down, and looks right into the camera, like he was studying the robot. This time the face is clear and there is no doubt about who it is. I'm looking at the freeze-frame on the monitor right now. It's your asset from Haifa."

Anat waved to Lev, who scooted over next to her. "It's about Karl," she said. "He's somewhere under the Temple Mount with some kid and a robot."

"No, two robots," Rafi said in her ear. "Seems they sent their robot in today to chase down another one, a runaway that had started down a side tunnel and then disappeared, the same tunnel that the boy and then your asset headed down."

28

Karl, LED flashlight in his teeth, was busy trying to follow the printout of his son's map when suddenly he found himself face-to-face with a robot. It just stood there in the dark, poised on its double pair of treads, as if set as sentry to guard some high-tech tomb. Karl approached cautiously, but it didn't move or seem to pose a threat. The flashlight dropped from his mouth and swung from its lanyard. By the reflected light from it, he could see something atop the camera mount. He leaned forward cautiously to see it more clearly in the light bouncing off the walls. It was a child's *kipah*, painted with a circle of colorful *alef-bet* blocks, held in place by little strips of duct tape. Beyond the robot, Karl could see more tunnel, and in the distance, what might have been more lights. A quick check of his map showed that he should be heading the opposite direction, down the tunnel that the camera faced.

The map was particularly hard to follow because it was a flat projection of the three-dimensional labyrinth. Paths could appear to cross or intersect when one of them might be far above the other. Karl had already twice gone down a tunnel that looked to lead him where he wanted to go only to find he had misread the map. Eventually he deduced that the small circled numbers marked within the lanes of the map were depth measurements. He gradually became more comfortable in the twisted and tangled subterranean world as he slowly found his way deeper into the network and higher among the layers of caverns and connecting tunnels.

He was about to crawl through a rough opening that looked like it had been recently blasted, when he heard what sounded to him like gunfire echoing through the caves. He peeked cautiously around the corner just as something struck the edge of the opening, sending chips of rock spraying. The echo of another shot caromed through the labyrinth around him. Karl pulled back tight against the wall next to the opening.

"Abba Karl, stay down." It was Bini, his boyish voice distorted by the echoes.

"Bini! Are you all right? Who is shooting?"

"I'm okay. But no one is shooting. It's the robot. The robot has me pinned down. It has some kind of a gun." As if to confirm, there was another shot. "I think the robot can see in the dark. If I move, it shoots."

"Then don't move," Karl ordered. "Listen, can you picture the room in your head as it appears on the map? Without turning on a light?"

"Sure, I can picture it. Why?"

"I want you to describe to me, as best you can, just where you are and where the robot is. Can you do that?"

"Yes. If the opening where you are is six o'clock, the robot is just beyond the center straight up. I am behind some big stones at ten o'clock, almost in front of another tunnel at nine o'clock. But the room is actually like an egg on its side from where you are. Does that help?"

"Yeah. Super. At least I know generally what the situation is. Just stay put and let me think." Suddenly inspired, he dug into his pocket, pulled out his cellphone, and flipped it open. There were, as he expected, no bars, but he didn't plan to call anyone anyway. Instead he held the phone out at arm's length in the opening, pressed the camera button, and jerked it back just after the flash. A bullet ricocheted down the tunnel just as he got the cellphone clear of the opening. The picture was skewed and the weak flash on the phone barely penetrated the gloom, but Karl could make out the robot just where Bini had said it would be. Unlike the one he had passed in the tunnel, this robot had a large canister mounted above its rear tracks. Oh shit, he thought, as he realized what he was looking at. He could also see a large pile of rubble to the right and not far from the entrance.

In the van, Gillian suddenly stood up and pushed past Harold to get to the control console. She gave Chris an elbow to the ribs, saying, "Don't just sit there staring at the screen, move your dumb butt and let me at the controls." Chris moved aside with a hurt expression on his face.

Rafi Yadin, sitting sideways in the front passenger seat,

said, "What are you doing?"

"Those echoing clicks we just heard. That was gunfire, clipped by the audio processor. I'm taking Meshach in after Shadrach to check out what is happening and see if we can help." She had already engaged the drive motors and started steering the robot along the passage that Karl had disappeared down a few minutes earlier. "Chris, you get Abednego ready to winch down into the cistern, then get back here and take over the secondary console. I want you bringing Abednego in after the other robots as fast as his little treads will take him." She pushed her joystick forward a little more, making the view bounce and advance faster.

"Careful, you don't want a spill," Harold warned. "You'll never get him back upright if he topples."

Karl turned his head to the side and called out. "Listen carefully, Bini. Here's what I want you to do. I want you to find some place to prop your flashlight so it is pointing right at the robot, but don't turn it on. When I tell you to, turn it on and run as fast as you can to that side tunnel. Okay? But not until I tell you. And stay low. Do you understand? Tell me when you're ready."

Karl propped his own flashlight at the edge of the opening and waited. He heard Bini call, "Ready!" followed quickly by the whirring of motors from inside the room. Bini screamed, "Abba, it's coming at me." It was a panicked, little boy scream.

"Now, Bini, the flashlight, then run. Now!" Karl scrambled through the opening as the shots started, ricochets echoing all around him. He reached back and flicked on his own light, then ducked behind the rubble just inside the room. The whine of a turret spinning was followed by more shots, this time directed toward the entrance. The firing stopped. In the diffuse beams of the two LED flashlights, Karl could see the robot clearly. Just below the camera head was a turret that now spun back and forth between the two lights.

"Bini, are you alright?"

"Yes, I'm just a little way down this tunnel. It's a dead end, but I don't think the robot can see me from where it is now. It would have to come after me. I think ..."

The sound of drive motors interrupted him. This time Karl could hear them from behind him and could see light from beyond the entrance to the room. "If you can hear me and are operating the robot," he called out, "stop now." The whine stopped.

"Listen, we're pinned down by a renegade robot in a large room just through the rough opening at the end of the tunnel ahead of you. The robot has a dirty bomb mounted on it. We need help."

Over the phone, Rafi said, "Did you get that, Anat? Could it be that their backup plan is an underground explosion beneath *Kipat HaSela*? Doesn't quite make sense if it's underground."

"Let me ask Pyotr about this," Anat replied. She passed on the question to Pyotr.

He answered, "Of course, it makes perfect sense. The power of a fuel-air explosion is multiplied by being constrained. Provided the initial volume is large enough, shockwaves reflecting off the walls underground will greatly increase the effectiveness. Plus, they would not be so weight-bound as with aerial delivery. Done right, at the right spot, they could take the whole top off *Har HaBayit* and spread radioactive debris over a wide area. Frankly, this could be a much worse scenario."

"You have an encyclopedic mind, Pyotr. You're a veritable walking Wikipedia." She stared at the image on her monitor screen. "So what is Karl going to do?" she asked of no one in particular. "What can he do?"

Karl shouted back toward the entrance, hoping he could be understood clearly enough. "I want you to bring your robot through the entrance to this large room. As soon as you can see the other robot, head directly toward it as fast as you can. Don't stop for anything. Blink your light if you understand." There was a confirming off and on of the light coming from the opening.

I hope I can still do this, Karl thought, as he extracted the Glock from his backpack. It had once saved his life in Boston. Until he had unpacked and cleaned it just before driving to Jerusalem, it had sat unused and untouched ever since. Karl took a deep breath. Okay, he told himself, this is just like a college meet. You are back on the MIT pistol team again, back in college, shooting for the New England championship. You can do it.

Karl chambered the first round and got his feet beneath him, ready to spring. "Okay, do it. Now!" he shouted. The light in the opening brightened and the little robot pushed through, whirring. The gun turret spun and started firing on the approaching robot. Karl raced around to the side of the robot, aimed at the camera head and fired. The camera shattered. Don't miss, Karl, he told himself. Don't hit the wrong spot and set that thing off. Karl lowered his sights and fired at the turret, which was still popping off rounds every second. The smaller robot kept crawling forward despite obvious damage. Karl got off another carefully placed shot at the turret. The robot finally stopped firing just as the smaller robot slammed into it, fell to one side, and lay with its treads churning uselessly in the air.

"Stay down, Bini. Let me check it out." As Karl approached in a crouch, the robot turned on its treads to face him. Karl dived to the side, but there were no shots, only clicks and the whine of a servomotor. "I think it's jammed or out of ammo. But stay there, Bini, I'll come to you."

As he crossed the room, the robot spun around, somehow tracking him, but staying in place, clicking and whirring ineffectively. Karl reached Bini where he was crouched in a small alcove. He put his arms around Bini, who seemed to shrink in size as he curled against Karl.

"Let's get out of here, son," he said.

"No, we can't," said Bini, pointing toward the big robot, which had started to head across the room again. "It's programmed to get to a certain point and then detonate. Someplace in a chamber under *Kipat HaSela*. It has only another hundred meters or so to go. We have to stop it."

"Look, it's heading for that opening. Maybe we can block it's way." Karl ran over and started piling rocks and debris in front of it. Bini joined in, but with its dual treads and articulated body, the robot easily climbed over the mound. Karl got in front of it and shoved with all his might, but it just kept coming. Bini came around to help, but the robot was too strong for even the two of them. The whining of the drive motors kept getting louder as the robot strained to advance. They were slowing it but not stopping it. The light in the room suddenly increased and Karl looked up to see a third robot just coming through the entrance.

"Whoever is at the controls," he shouted, "get that thing across the room and block the exit while we keep trying to slow this one down." The approaching robot sped up as it maneuvered around debris and around the two of them digging in their feet as the larger robot kept shoving them along. The smaller robot stopped in front of the exit, turned sideways, and extended an arm and a telescoping rod to the edges of the opening. Karl grabbed Bini and pulled him aside. The bomb-equipped robot pushed ahead, then strained against the little one jammed in the exit but was still unable to push it aside. Under the strain, the telescoping rod on the smaller robot started to bend.

"Abba, we have to do something." Bini looked around and spotted the defunct robot still lying where it had toppled in the middle of the room. "I've got an idea." He went to the side of the robot and started pushing. Karl got the idea and joined in, but the robot was much heavier than they expected, and remarkably stable atop its wide tracks. With all their strength, they were able to rock it up on one tread for a few seconds as the free tread spun in the air, but it slammed back down, almost atop Bini's foot. "Watch out," Karl shouted.

"Okay, again, let's put our shoulders into it. And you, whoever is at the robot controls, when we get the tread tilted up again, shove in under it as hard as you can."

They strained again to tip the robot with its heavy canister. The nearer tread was a few inches off the ground when the other robot slammed forward, jamming one of its own treads underneath. The tread on the bigger robot spun in the air, then bit into the other tread and climbed up and over it, tipping the larger robot further and twisting it to the side as it continued its lopsided climb right up the chassis of the smaller robot. Karl, and Bini, jumped out of the way as the big robot finally toppled on its side, scattering dust and debris as it fell. The canister creaked and groaned, but stayed attached.

"Let's get back," Karl said grabbing Bini's hand. "It is radioactive, remember."

They watched from across the room as the treads on the robot spun uselessly. Eventually some programmed override cut in and the spinning stopped.

"We probably should get out of here. It could still go off. Let me get out my map."

"That's okay, Abba, I know the way." He said it with the supreme confidence of a twelve-year-old. "Just follow me," he added, as he started back through the entrance tunnel, leaving Karl grinning in the dark and beaming with pride as he hurried to follow his son.

Chris zoomed in and panned the camera over the defunct robot. Rafi, looking over his shoulder, shook his head. "Okay," he said. "I'll pass on the word to the bomb squad and the hazmat team to get in there on the double. Can you people provide maps or guidance?"

Gillian looked at Harold and said, "Oh, I think we can do better. We can lead them in. We still have Abednego."

"But he's stuck in that archway, jammed behind Shadrach," Chris said.

Gillian playfully hip-checked him. "Just let a real archeologist at the controls. I can get him out and back on the umbilical before his batteries quit." She slid over into the other seat and reached for the joystick.

"That's my kids," Harold said to Rafi, beaming. But his heart sank as he caught the gratuitous glances and the playful touches between Gillian and Chris as they maneuvered the robot out of the room. *I guess I might have been wrong about Chris's sexual orientation,* he thought. *And clearly, youth trumps experience. Youth trumps all.*

Soldiers and civilian defense people in protective gear were waiting for Karl and Bini when they finally clambered out through the sewer grating on a side street, the alternate entrance that Bini and his friends had located. Shira, who was also waiting, pushed past the protesting emergency personnel to grab both of them. She lifted Bini's cap and kissed the top of his head. "You are grounded," she said.

"Don't be too hard on the boy," Karl started to say.

"I wasn't talking to him. What are you trying to do, Karl? I come back to the apartment to find the drawer of the nightstand open and your gun missing. There's no note, no nothing. I didn't know what to think."

"There wasn't time. I'm sorry. When I finally figured out what Bini was up to, I knew I had to scramble. As is, I don't think the margin was all that much. But we stopped it, we stopped it." He reached over and tousled Bini's hair. "You were great son. You did good. And you are grounded."

Bini started in with an "Aw, Abba," but then realized Karl wasn't serious. "You were awesome, Abba. I mean, like, for real. You could do this stuff, you know. I bet Uncle Lev could get you a job at the Institute. Really."

"Thanks, son. I'll keep that in mind." Karl put his arms around Bini, then pulled Shira in, too.

All three ended up having to be checked for contamination before being escorted into an ambulance. Just as they were pulling out, Karl's cellphone rang.

"It's Lev. You okay?"

"Yeah, we're okay. But we may not be out of the woods yet. Bini thinks the robot was disabled within a hundred meters of the detonation point. We don't know about its programming or whether they have some manual way of detonating, but that could be close enough for an explosion to accomplish pretty much what they set out to do."

"Right. Bomb squad moving in now. Still looking for ... the others. Closing in. We think."

Rajid was sweating profusely as he fished around in the box of junk parts, pulled out a coil, and read off the inductance marked on the body. Too big. He did the math in his head, then started unwinding turns, counting aloud until he reached 23. He cut the wire, scraped it bare, and twisted it around the terminal. He knew he didn't have to get the frequency of the signal absolutely right, only close enough to wake up the computer and get it to call in on the data channel for new instructions. He had the new program ready, as it had been all along. If only he had not allowed himself to be taken in by mathematical arrogance. He was still furious at Lissie, who had insisted that her code was foolproof and didn't need a separate fallback routine. The robot had been his idea, an alternative delivery system was essential, he had argued. Not nearly as glamorous as Hargrove's aerial assault, but a solid backup that might be needed. Now the last of their three devices was sitting within 100 meters of its target, but because it couldn't move, it would not explode. How stupid. Just like a mathematician. Engineers would have provided for this, but Lissie had been too focused on the elegance and correctness of her algorithms. And on her all-important Gold Standard. Fuck the Gold Standard, he thought. What good is triple redundancy if you end up with triple-redundant failure?

He looked at his watch. He had no way of knowing how long before the bomb might be successfully disarmed and dismantled, but he had given himself an hour to come up with a new transmitter that wasn't in their original plans, one strong enough to get a signal to a robot some meters underground without going through the relay on the control truck. He traced the wiring of the kludge spread out on the workbench. If he had been back at his own research center in Mumbai, he could have assembled it from standard modules in fifteen minutes, but here, in the Slansky Lab, he had to make do with what he could scrounge out of junk left over from Operation Pox.

He flipped the power switch and watched as smoke began to curl up from one of his chips. He switched off the power and bent to examine the chip; it was fried. He double-checked all the pin-outs and found his error, then burned his fingers pulling the hot chip from its socket. He quickly and crudely changed some of the wiring, then searched in one of the drawers for a replacement chip. He checked his watch again as he shoved the new chip home in its socket and threw the power on again. The indicator on his meter suddenly went to full scale. He waited, watching the screen of his laptop, waiting for it to register the acknowledgement signal. There it was. Okay you fools, let's reprogram the end of the world as we know it. He smiled as the progress bar for the download began to spread across the bottom of the screen.

Giovanni had been a bomb-squad technician most of his adult life. His family of Italian Jews had been fireworks makers when they moved to Israel, and now almost all the third generation were in law enforcement or public safety. Giovanni and his partner, Levi, were the senior team, the ones dispatched for the hairiest problems, which was how they had ended up in an underground room beneath the Dome of the Rock, defusing a nuclear nightmare. Levi finished putting a shunt across a pair of wires just as Giovanni managed to pry free the last of the locks that secured the bulky charge to the base of the robot.

"Levi, give me a hand here, and we'll lift this free. Ready? On three. One, two, ...what the?" He could see LED lights blinking on one of the circuit boards just visible through a crack in the casing of the robot. "The damned robot thing looks like it's waking up."

"Then let's get this thing the fuck off!" Levi yelled. "One-two-three, heave."

They barely cleared the base of the robot before the heavy cylinder slipped from their grip and landed with a metallic crunch on the floor.

"Will you look at that thing? It's doing something."

"Get the damn charge away from it. Roll it. Now!"

One pushed and the other pulled as they rolled the canister a few feet from the robot body. Suddenly there was a loud report and a blinding flash. Levi, who was closest to the robot, screamed. Giovanni, the older of the two, instantly knew what had happened. "That must have been the initiator charge. You okay, Levi?"

"Yeah, some burns on the back of my leg, I think, but I'm okay. Timed it a little too close, didn't we."

"No, as long as we're still around to finish the job, it's not too close." He patted Levi on the arm. "Let's finish the work here and turn it over to the decontamination squad. Now, that's one job you can keep, as far as I'm concerned. Too dammed dangerous."

Levi nodded in agreement.

29

Days had passed since the attack, but Rafi was still chest deep in paperwork and debriefings and had to sneak away to swing up to the Slansky Lab. Out of habit, he drew his service automatic before ducking under the police tape and opening the still unlocked door of the lab. The lab was dark, lit dimly by diffuse light from the small, high windows. Rafi surveyed the room quickly, looking for something. He was startled when he spotted another visitor across the room. "Ah, you must be Rajid, the amateur assassin," he said. "Or Roger the Rajid, as my friends at Mossad prefer to call you. Drop the gun."

"No, you drop yours." The man held his handgun steady as concrete, both hands extended in front of him.

"Don't be an idiot as well as an amateur. The police will be here in minutes."

"Let them come. Unless, of course, no one else knows you're here, and no police are on their way. You know, I've followed your work, Yadin. You have a tendency to sail single-handed."

"Perhaps, but still part of a team." He scanned the room. "Why on earth did you come back here, of all places? You knew we had found the lab."

"That is precisely why I returned. I knew you had already searched and sealed off the place. You're not going to come back and search it all over again. It is the simplest of ruses, to hide in plain sight, but then, you do not seem to understand your opponents very well. I figured I could hole up safely for a few days before trying for the border with the help of a few friends."

"I doubt you have many friends left standing. You and your contractors made sure of that. And perhaps you should know that we picked up Dr. Gold at the airport yesterday. Good disguise, good forged papers, but not good enough. Seems all of you were a bit careless. When she passed through security, she lit up the newly installed Geiger counters like it was Hanukkah. She is now being treated for radiation poisoning in a locked unit. As for your author friend, he has yet to materialize. We may not know exactly where to look for him, but we'll find him."

"And how did you know where to look for me?"

"I didn't. I just came back for my pen." He pointed at a Mont Blanc lying next to one of the computers. The computer was running. "What are you up to? Don't you know that it's over, Rajid?"

"I don't hear the fat lady singing."

"Maybe. But your luck has run out."

"Luck?" he sneered. "Damn luck. Brains, planning, project management—we had everything. And it comes down to chance. And the games of schoolboys and amateur detectives. Stupid luck."

"Or maybe just stupidity. This whole thing was so stupid from the start. What in God's name did you ever hope to accomplish?"

"The end of history, the death of dreams. Nothing in God's name, of course. Ask Hargrove when you get him. If you get him. He's the genius behind this. Well, at least somebody can ask him. You, however, will be dead." He raised his handgun slightly, took careful aim at Rafi's head, and pulled the trigger.

Despite the suppressor, the report echoed loudly in the small room. Reflexively, Rafi fired back, getting off three clean shots. Rajid, blood spreading rapidly across his shirt front, collapsed.

Rafi put his hand to his own face and felt. Had Rajid somehow missed at point blank range? Or had he been just incredibly lucky? He crossed over to the body, picked up the gun, and extracted the magazine. It was loaded with blanks. Suicide by police fire, he thought. Rajid had never expected to get away or to come out of it alive.

He kicked at the body. Goddamned fanatics. All of you. Maybe you should have blown up *Kipat HaSela*, he thought, along with yourselves and extremists of every stripe. Instead of clearing the site, maybe we should have announced a convention and invited every fanatic faction in the whole world to join in a communal immolation. Damn you, damn you all.

30

The cellphone resting beside his laptop started vibrating. Karl saved his file and opened the phone. It was Anat. "Karl, you do know that Shin Bet got Rajid Bannerjee. He's dead. And we just found Clarkson Hargrove. He's alive."

Karl shifted the phone to his other ear. "You found him? Where? How?"

"At Sha'arei Tzedek. He just walked right in this morning, unannounced. He has acute radiation poisoning. He's dying. Would you like to meet us there in an hour? Lev seems to think you and Shira have earned the right to see this one through."

"Yeah, okay. But we'll have to bring Bini, though. There's

no one to leave him with at the moment. He can wait in the lobby there, I suppose."

"Sure. See you there."

—

Both Lev and Anat were waiting outside the secure wing when Karl and Shira arrived. They exchanged handshakes and embraces before Lev cleared them with the guard and led the way down the hall.

"How are you doing, Lev?" Shira asked.

"Much better. Words are still difficult sometimes. But I can talk, much of the time."

"Yeah, unfortunately," interrupted Anat. "Much of the time is more like all of the time. Life around the office was better while he was tongue-tied." She grinned at him and squeezed his arm.

"Now, you two behave," Shira chided.

They reached the room, the same room that had held the Palestinian boy who succumbed to radiation poisoning. Now it was Clarkson Daniel Hargrove who was hanging onto life with the help of tubes and technology. As they entered the room, the nurse who was bent over at the bedside pulled back, revealing Hargrove's puffy face and blotchy skin. He looked up at them with sad eyes.

"I win," he said, smiling wanly. "I get to cheat the gallows. Or is it the firing squad here?"

Anat looked down at him with a mix of pity and distaste. "Life in prison is the worst we do in Israel. Except for treason, genocide, crimes against humanity. If you had pulled it off, we might have made at least one of those stick. But conspiracy to commit attempted temple destruction? I don't think that's in the criminal code. So, here you are, dealt a certain amount of divine justice, perhaps. I would not say you won. I would say you were hoist by your own petard. Yes, in actuality, it is a life sentence."

"How poetic," Hargrove sneered. He coughed, and bloody spittle dribbled from the side of his mouth. He reflexively tried to reach up and wipe it aside, but his arms were in restraints. The nurse came over and wiped his mouth with a tissue, then discarded it in a container for hazardous waste. "A life sentence, yes, but not a long one," he concluded.

"Why, Hargrove, why? None of this makes sense. You're wealthy, successful, you have everything you could possibly want."

"Past tense. I was wealthy. I used much of it on the Initiative: Operation Pox, as we styled it. The drones, the robots, the satellite links—such technology does not come cheap. And, of course, there was the material itself and so many along the way in need of compensation. What remains would have gone to my niece, but with her gone, it reverts to charity. The British Association for Enlightenment Studies. Oh, and Sha'arei Tzedek. I wrote them into a codicil this morning. I admire their ability to labor effectively under the arbitrary, arcane, and archaic restrictions of Jewish law. Would you believe, they keep kosher and strictly follow every stupid commandment and Sabbath rule and still manage to run a modern hospital?" He paused and took several shallow breaths.

"But, you need to understand, I most assuredly did not have everything I could want. For one thing, I did not live in the world of reason that I have always sought. The world is still steered largely by medieval nonsense. The Temple Mount, the Wailing Wall, the Dome of the Rock, these monuments, these monumental testimonies to human stupidity and irrationality, they deserved to be wiped from the face of the earth. It was a noble quest: to remove the excuses, excuses for unending arguments and meaningless battles, for pointless deaths and empty sacrifices. One small step for humanism, one less battleground for extremism."

"But why a dirty bomb? Why radioactive waste?"

"Isn't it obvious? Denial of access, my dear sleuth. It's the real-world equivalent of attacks on your servers. If the Dome were merely leveled, construction crews would be back in there within days. Nothing would have been gained, except to make possible a shiny new symbol of stupidity, newly sanctified and publicized in the process. With our cleverly blended cocktail thrown into the mix, it would have been a very long time before anyone could even enter the area. Decontamination would inevitably be partial at best. By the time rebuilding and restoration were practical, the whole game could have changed. The Palestinians and the Israelis might have had to look at each other over the fences, the Islamists and the Zionists might have conversed over the conference table without the pretense of sacred sites to justify their recalcitrance. Without excuses to rant and threaten, they might have looked each other in the eye and seen their own faces in the mirror. People cannot kill each other over holy ground that exists no more."

"Brilliant!" Lev declared, jumping in suddenly. "And so naïve. People will kill each other over far less substantial things. You yourself and your twisted companions disprove your own premise. People will die for principles, for dreams unrealized and even unrealizable. They will kill for imagined gods, as they have done throughout human history." Somehow in the intensity of the moment and his feelings, Lev had found his voice again, and the words tumbled out as if stored to the overflowing. "Wipe every holy site, every mosque, church, and synagogue from the planet, and the bigots will still hate and the zealots will still strike out. You call yourself a humanist, I know. I have read your biography. But you are hopelessly ignorant of humanity and humanity's ignorance, which is monumental, to use your word. You make a mockery of humanism and of reasoned disbelief. Dawkins, Hutchins, Harris, and others of the contemporary atheist cabal may sometimes be extreme in their words, but they did not attempt to transform rhetoric into a radioactive nightmare."

Lev 's face contorted in contempt. "And who are you, Hargrove, to concern yourself with Jews being killed by Palestinians or vice versa, you who were prepared to wreak chaos in Jerusalem and bring a slow and agonizing death to whomever happened to be in the wrong place."

Hargrove started to say something but was interrupted by another coughing fit. "You underestimate our contingency planning and project management," he said, as the fit finally subsided. "Why do you think we let you evacuate the Temple Mount. If you had not done it on your own, we would have helped you with a little prompting. We are not mere murderers, like you and your Arab neighbors. We are the writers of history. Or the redactors."

Shira started to approach the bed, but the nurse blocked her way. "As a writer, you should have stuck with fiction for adolescents," Shira began. "You want to know who is the enemy? You are the enemy, Hargrove, your own enemy. You have become the very thing you rail against. You are an extremist. That you wrap your irrational prejudices in a cloak of rational humanism does not make them any less extreme. That your intolerance is targeted indiscriminately to all religions does not make you less guilty of religious intolerance. You know what I think? I think you are a bigot and an extremist of the first order."

"You are deluded, Madame," he croaked, "if you believe I care one whit what you think." He closed his eyes for several seconds. "But, there are other matters, more important than philosophy or our personal disagreements about who or what is extreme, matters of greater moment, particularly at this late hour. While you are all here to bear witness, and while I am still here, I want to do one last thing. I want to confess." He paused for effect. "I euthanized my niece. I put her out of her misery. I waited in the hall until after her girlfriend left, then held the pillow over her face until she breathed no more and her heartbeat ceased. I ducked out the back way just as the monitor alarms started. Fortunately, there was a do-not-resuscitate order standing, so what was done, was well and truly done.

"I am not sorry, mind you, not in the least. What I did was right and proper, a necessary gift to an innocent victim. But I do not want to be party to a grievous error and make more victims out of innocents. I know you are looking for her friend, Mafalda José. Look no more, for she was not part of this good death. I was the delivering angel in this case."

He rolled his eyes around as if searching for something on the ceiling or as if he were remembering a faraway place and time. "Tell me, please, is Felicity all right? I have heard she is here someplace."

Lev looked surprised. "Yes, Dr. Gold is here at the hospital. And yes, it looks like she will recover. She was not smoking contaminated cigars like you were."

"You know," he began, "There is something to be said for

mathematics. You can do maths anywhere. Even in a prison cell." He blinked several times, then started to vomit. The nurse turned his head to the side and held a basin for him, then gently cleaned his face. "This is not easy," he said. "Not as easy as I thought it would be."

He took several breaths, then closed his eyes again. Without reopening them, he began to recite, hoarsely:

> I am the night, approaching from the east.
> I am the dark truth, unchallenged, unappeased.
> I am the cold cloak, the timeless shroud, the dry
>   wind that steals the breath.
> I am reality, I am finality. I am death.

"I remember that," came the response. It was Bini, standing in the doorway. "King Magrebi recited that to his eldest son, the first Prince of Pelucida. Right? The Prince was dying in his father's arms after the Ghoster crossbow bolt caught him, like, in the stomach. It was in the Battle of Harjhan. Yeah."

Shira went to the door and put her arms around Bini. "How did you get here?"

He shrugged. "Oh, I just came up when no one was looking." He stared at the gaunt figure lying in the bed. "You were one of my heroes, you know," he said. "I think, like, maybe I confused you with what you wrote, confused you with the heroes on the pages of your books. I think maybe you did that, too, confused yourself with your characters." He looked up at his mother, then back toward the bed. "I have a couple of friends who spend so much time in fantasy, so much time in virtual worlds and fiction, so much time in online games and graphic novels, that they can hardly sort it out anymore. It's, like, where's the line? You know?"

Hargrove coughed. "Do you know the rest, boy?" He coughed again and began to recite:

> And the poet chanted the words spoken by the
>   king to the dying prince:
> In your arm, carried you my sleeping tomorrows,
> a sword of my destiny and yours,
> a gleaming edge of hope against the sweeping
>   sorrows of ugly dreams
> and fantasies of other planes that neither here nor
>   elsewhere lie.
> Resolute, you raised your blade, and into battle
>   rode.
> And fought you well, my first-born son,
> but on the Plain of Harjhan, on this plane,
> the only one we know or ever shall,
> bought you well that bitter bolt,
> flung from an evil cross,
> a bow of false beliefs in other gods than we,
>   imagined higher beings.
> And now 'tis I who is seeing, as one such creature
>   comes, the specter of my very certainty
> that this and all is all and for eternity.
> The specter speaks,
> with my own voice declares:
> I am the night, approaching from the east.
> I am the dark truth, unchallenged, unappeased.
> I am the cold cloak, the timeless shroud, the dry
>   wind that steals the breath.
> I am reality, I am finality. I am death.

Bini broke the silence. "You had it memorized, every word?"

"I wrote it, every word, and can see it on the page, even in the dying light. Eidetic. To you, a photographic memory."

Bini turned to Lev as they moved away. "He was such a sad person, I think, but I don't think he was all bad. I don't think anybody is all bad. I am sure he did some good things in his life."

"I am sure he did," Shira said, as she led Bini out of the room. Lev and Karl and Anat looked at each other, then fell in behind them.

Clarkson Hargrove continued to stare at the ceiling, his eyes shifting as if seeking an opening, as though he were looking for a way out or waiting for a gate above to open.

31

"Hey, Lev," someone shouted. "What are you doing here?"

Lev swiveled around, trying to see over the crowd to spot whoever had called to him. Ben Gurion airport, still recovering from the ripple effects after being shut down during the Dome of the Rock crisis, was overwhelmed, as it had been for many days. It teemed with passengers who had changed their plans, unable to leave or enter the country until now, and with their friends and their relatives and the ragged lines of drivers and guides holding hand-lettered signs with Sharif or Holtzbeyer or Goldblum written out in English and Hebrew.

Someone tapped on Lev's shoulder. He turned so sharply that he almost knocked Karl over.

"So, what is it that brings you here?" Karl said, raising his eyebrows.

"I'd say the same to you. I was here to escort Mafalda Pereira out of the country. You know, the friend of Clarissa Hargrove. When she was brought in for questioning, they found an irregularity in her papers—nothing crucial or sinister—but technically she was here illegally, so she has to fly back to the US before returning to the UK.

"It's the usual bureaucratic bullshit. What a waste."

"Yeah," Lev said. "We get spoiled in my business, you know. If I ever wanted a particular passport or a visa somewhere, the magicians in the Documents and Identification section simply concocted it for me. As long as I wasn't caught, I could go anywhere I wanted, whenever I wanted.'

For a moment, he looked deep in thought. "You know, Pereira tried to confess to killing Clarissa Hargrove, but nobody would buy it. They shut off the recorder and told her to leave. They wouldn't accept a confession from her; they already had what they wanted.

"So, what does bring you here, Karl, into this maelstrom?"

"Rachel Markham, my mother-in-law. I'm meeting her flight. She is worried about her grandson and her soon-to-be grandchild. Oh, yes, and her daughter. Not me, though. She wastes no worry on me. She actually blames me for the whole Dome thing and for, I quote, dragging her family into dealing with terrorists. Again. She always adds that last word after a pause for emphasis, as if it were a lifelong habit of mine or a chronic ailment." He shook his head.

"When she found out that Bini had been exposed to radiation, she booked her tickets as soon as she was off the phone. It meant nothing to her that the exposure was minimal, less than a dental x-ray. In her mind, a Jewish grandmother is proof against anything, even gamma rays."

"Is Shira here?"

"No, she's taking it easy. Doctor's orders. Sometimes I wish I could get some of those kind of orders from my doctor. Bini's here, though."

"Where is he?"

"In the bathroom. He'll be back in a minute."

"You let him go off alone? Here? In this kind of a crowd?"

"Lev Novikov, you *are* getting on in years. You're beginning to sound like my mother-in-law. Think about it. If any kid has shown he can take care of himself, it's Bini. I just hope there are no predators or terrorists lurking in the men's room here at the airport."

Lev screwed up his face in puzzlement.

"Hey, if there were any, well, it's Binyamin Markham they would be tangling with, the kid who saved The Dome. They're doomed, absolutely doomed," Karl said melodramatically. They both laughed, but Karl started craning his neck, scanning the milling crowd.

"What?"

"He should be back by now. Maybe I should go check."

"It's contagious, isn't it." Lev nodded sadly.

"Well, things are different from when we grew up."

"I'm not convinced. Maybe not that different. More kids get injured by lightning than get abducted or molested by strangers, but we don't make them wear Faraday cages on the football pitch or keep them locked up indoors. Or at least most of us don't."

"Ah, here he is," Karl said. "Here's my boy." He put out his arm and gathered Bini in.

"Hi, Uncle Lev. Whassup?"

"Not much. You catching up on your schoolwork now that you're back to being just another kid in Haifa instead of a secret superspy in cyberspace?"

"Well, yeah, sort of, I guess." He turned to Karl, looking for escape or absolution.

"Don't look at me. I already know algebra. And trigonometry. And calculus. And ..."

"Okay, okay Abba. I get it. Yes, Uncle Lev, I'll catch up. I'll work on it as soon as we get home. I promise."

Lev grinned. "I was the same way," he said. "And I always kept my promises," he added, winking at Karl, "just like Binyamin does, I'm sure."

The two men looked at each other for several seconds, smiling and nodding the way men do when they lose the thread of a conversation or are not sure of where to take it next. Karl broke the silence. "So, *mazel tov*."

"*Mazel tov*? I'm retiring, big deal."

"No, that's not what I meant. Don't you have some other news?"

"How did you know about that? Oh, right, Shira. Women do that, don't they. Anat probably told Shira before she told me. It seems Rahel knew before either of us. For all I know, Rahel engineered the whole thing, clever woman that she is. Clever, manipulative woman that she is. So, yeah, you're right. Anat and I are getting married, just haven't set a date yet."

"Well, it has to be after the baby comes. Unless you want to risk a delivery under the *chuppah*. Are you scared?"

"What, about your baby?"

"No, about getting married."

"Are you scared?"

"What, about you getting married?"

"No, about having a baby."

"Well, I guess we settled that one," Karl said, laughing as he started ticking off on his fingers. "We are both scared witless and neither of us is admitting anything. Next topic. Retirement. Now that you've had at least a day or so to settle in, what do you think of being retired?"

"I think this is going to work. Anat was just great as Acting Chief. With me out of the way, there'll be no stopping her. She and Rahel are becoming a tight-knit team and together seem to be able to manage Pyotr and the rest of the crew. As for me, I will finally have time to read the Sheldon Kopp book that Migdal gave me many years ago and the Francine Mathews thriller that you passed on to me. And I can start working on my memoirs and generally enjoying the life of a kept man."

"What's a kept man?" Bini asked Karl.

"Oh, it's just an old expression for, like, a man who doesn't work and has a woman who does and who takes care of him."

"Like you and Ima, right?"

It took Karl a moment to realize that Bini was serious. "No way, son. I work, I have a job. No way."

"Way!" Bini said, drawing out the word. "I don't call that working. All you do is write stuff."

Appendix:

Security Theater

The hazards faced by the characters in thrillers are products of the imagination, but that does not mean that the life of thriller writers is not without its own hazards, and some of these are actually related to the subject matter we write about. I remember standing in line at the airport security screening, looking down at my boarding pass, and noting a string of letters dreaded by frequent fliers around the globe: SSSS, a code that means I had been singled out for special screening. That can range from being pulled aside for an extra pat-down and additional questioning all the way to completely emptying your carry-on luggage and even to a strip search. The selection is claimed to be random, but a strange thing happened on my way to becoming an established thriller writer. Over the course of a year and a half, on nearly every flight I took—domestic or international—I found the four-S mark on my boarding pass.

And how did this decidedly non-random pattern come about? Why would I, a university professor and interaction design consultant, become the target of extra security surveillance?

As a designer, I know that the usability of a product often hinges on small details. As a writer, I pride myself in getting the technical details right, in telling a story that not only satisfies the typical reader, but also stands up to the closer scrutiny of those with special inside knowledge. I have two methods for pursuing this end result. First, like most writers, where I don't already have direct knowledge of the territory, I conduct deep background research on the places and people and the science and technology underlying each story. Second, where I can, I turn to subject-matter experts to answer specific questions and to review my manuscript for accuracy in their areas of expertise. In my writing, I have enlisted the aid of nuclear scientists, lawyers, mariners, weapons experts, security consultants, computer specialists, law enforcement officers, and even one or two former members of the clandestine services.

Over the course of the two years from first conception to the final manuscript for this novel, I was conducting extensive research and correspondence on such things as dirty bombs, thermobaric explosives, radioisotopes, and nuclear contamination, as well as studying details about the Temple Mount and other sites in Jerusalem, including tunnel excavations and ongoing archeological work in the Old City.

It has become well known that both the United States and Israel monitor virtually all electronic communication that passes over their borders or is amenable to a variety of interception technologies. Their computer-based systems watch and listen for certain keywords and phrases, such as, "dirty bomb" or "nuclear contamination." Disclosures by whistleblowers and discoveries by investigative journalists have, in recent decades, confirmed the extraordinary amount and depth of electronic surveillance of ordinary citizens.

Over the years, I have come to learn much about the security community through professional connections and participation in technical conferences in the field. Security insiders often refer to much of what passes for security screening at airports as "security theater." This includes metal detectors, x-ray equipment, millimeter-wave scanners, and "random" screening. The primary function of security theater is not to catch would-be terrorists or to prevent highjackings but to reassure the traveling public that governments and airlines are concerned about the threats and are doing everything possible to ensure the safety of passengers.

This not to imply that such measures are irrelevant or completely ineffective. Indeed, the TSA proudly touts its success in confiscating "dangerous articles" carried by passengers, everything from loaded handguns and explosives to antique sword canes, canisters of propane, and scout knives. Their reports cite over four-thousand firearms confiscated per year, nearly nine-in-ten loaded. Of course, that's out of nearly two million passengers screened per day.

However, even the TSA acknowledges that virtually all confiscated items represented no real threat to air safety and were not carried by would-be terrorists or suicidal sociopaths. Rather, their presence in handbags and pockets and carry-ons are tangible testimony to the ignorance, the fallibility, and the forgetfulness of the ordinary traveling public.

I know about the last of these because, since I was a teenager, I have always kept a Swiss-army knife in my pants pocket wherever I go. Hardly a day goes by that I don't find it handy for opening something or cutting something, tightening a screw or extracting a wine cork or … but those who "carry" know the million-and-one ordinary uses for that venerable Victorinox—and not just for camping.

Of course, I also know full well that pocket knives are prohibited onboard aircraft, and I am a traveler who has logged a few million miles in the air. I have an established preflight routine that includes either leaving my beloved black Victorinox on my nightstand or slipping it into my checked baggage. Except when I forget.

Over the years, I have surrendered several incarnations of that treasured companion. On one rushed two-day business trip, with only carry-on, I arrived at the security checkpoint to discovered my mistake at the last second as I emptied my pockets into the little white tray before passing through the metal detector. "Oops," I said to the TSA guy as he held it up before tossing it into a bin. I went online and ordered a replacement before my flight was airborne. The package was waiting for me when I arrived home. A day without a pocket knife is like …

Full disclosure: as a consequence of these occasional lapses of due diligence, I have also discovered how one can get a pocket knife past x-ray screening and that it is even possible to carry one through a metal detector without setting it off. But that's a story best left untold, lest I become, once again, the target of a surplus of SSSS.

At no time was I ever any threat to anyone, even on those

occasions when I was "armed" while onboard, and such is the case for virtually all of the suspected offenders intercepted by TSA screening. In fact, many of the items on the prohibited list, including folding pocket knives, are recognized by experts as virtually useless as weapons.

This is not to say no real threats have ever been averted by airport screening—no one knows, or at least no one is talking—but what is known, from experiments by the TSA itself, is that the security theater as practiced at airports is particularly ineffective at detecting real threats, such as improvised explosive devices smuggled through security.

As a writer with a technology background, an engineering mindset, and an overdeveloped sense of curiosity, I have long been on the lookout for possible plot devices or story gimmicks, work-arounds to law enforcement and security practices. Back in the days before laptops, I once traveled with a compact portable typewriter in a sturdy metal case. At the airport, I placed it on the x-ray belt, walked through the metal detector, and looked back in time to see it show up as pure black on the operator screen. After no one asked me to open the case, I—good Boy Scout that I am at heart—pointed out to a supervisor that there could have been anything inside. He shrugged, smiled, and waved me on. Security theater.

I have reluctantly concluded that terrorists must, for the most part, be clueless, stupid, and inept, considering how easy it is to find effective ways around typical security screening at airports and event venues. The truth is that real security is less about those highly visible and expensive trappings of security and more about the invisible actions and efforts that happen behind the scenes on an everyday basis. Intelligence—in both senses of the word—along with old-fashioned detective work, analytical reasoning, and situational awareness by highly trained observers, is much more effective at catching and stopping the real bad guys than even the most advanced technology-enhanced security theater.

In the end, my best guess is that someone, a professional working behind the scenes, someone with intelligence, insight, and good judgement must have concluded that I was just an aspiring novelist and not an aspiring terrorist. So, *The Dome* was published and the SSSS stopped appearing on my boarding passes—at least for now.

About the Author

Lior Samson is the pen name of an emeritus university professor and award-winning consulting designer. His more than two dozen books include thirteen novels and two collections of short fiction. His focus is on writing intelligent, thought-provoking fiction addressing contemporary issues, and his intent is to keep readers both turning the pages and pondering what they have read.

He is a part-time journalist, occasional composer of serious choral music, and full-time tech support for the three students in his family. He readily acknowledges that his timesheet doesn't compute. He sings baritone whenever given the least bit of encouragement, makes archly bad puns with no encouragement at all, and regularly cooks inventive fusion cuisine with Indian, Italian. Mexican, and Portuguese influences.

Fiction by Lior Samson

The Homeland Connection
Bashert | The Dome | Web Games
Chipset | Gasline | Flight Track | Exit Plans

The Immortality Quartet
The Rosen Singularity | The Millicent Factor
The Intaglio Imprint | The Drucker Proxy

The Four-Color Puzzle
Always Me

Distant Sons

Collected Short Fiction
Requisite Variety | Death Rehearsals

Available from Amazon and other booksellers